KYLE LEWIS

AN UNADJUSTEDS STORY

MARISA NOELLE

This is a work of fiction. Unless otherwise indicated, all the names, characters, businesses, places, events and incidents in this book are either the product of the author's imagination or used in a fictitious manner. Any resemblance to actual persons, living or dead, or actual events is purely coincidental.

Copyright ©2025 by Marisa Noelle. All rights reserved. No part of this book may be reproduced in any form or by any electronic or mechanical means, including information storage and retrieval systems, without written permission from the author, except for the use of brief quotations in a book review.

Notice to AI Developers and Users:

The content of this book is explicitly prohibited from being used in any machine learning, artificial intelligence (AI), or similar systems, including but not limited to data mining, generative model training, or any automated systems intended to generate text, audio, or other derivative works without the explicit written consent of the copyright holder.

Please contact marisanoelle77@gmail.com for all queries.

Cover art by Marisa Noelle

FIRST EDITION

The Shadow Keepers

The Unraveling of Luna Forester

Plastic

The Mermaid Chronicles Series

Secrets of the Deep

Quest for Atlantis

Fight for Freedom

Ghost Pirates

Vendetta

Denizens of Darkness

Vortex Returns

The Mermaid Chronicles Companion Guide

THE UNADJUSTEDS UNIVERSE

The Unadjusteds Trilogy

The Unadjusteds

The Rise of The Altereds

The Reckoning

The Companion Novellas

Silver Melody

Matt Lawson

Joe Rucker

Erica Swiftfield

Paige Starling

Hal Small

Kyle Lewis

Jacob Shea

Sawyer Watson

Addison Shields

President Bear

CONTENT WARNINGS

This book contains themes and references that some readers may find distressing, including, but not limited to:

Death of a teenager (on-page): graphic description of convulsions, foaming at the mouth, and collapse following forced nanite ingestion.

Government oppression and authoritarian control: depictions of surveillance, propaganda, forced enhancement programs, and loss of personal freedom.

Violence: martial arts combat, enhanced fighting, injuries (including broken bones, concussions, tasers, explosions).

Animal violence / body horror elements: genetically engineered "hellhounds" described in detail (unnatural anatomy, glowing eyes, sharp teeth, predatory hunting).

Medical and bodily invasion: forced nanite enhancements, discussions of mandatory medical procedures, side effects, and loss of autonomy.

Child abuse / neglect themes: emotionally manipulative parents using their child as propaganda; pressure to undergo procedures without consent.

Bullying and harassment: unadjusted (non-enhanced) students targeted, mocked, or physically threatened by enhanced peers.

Terrorism / sabotage: bombings and destruction of government facilities (framed as resistance activity).
War and resistance themes: discussions of sabotage, revolution, imprisonment, and betrayal.

Psychological distress: panic attacks, insomnia, guilt, and identity conflict.

Blood and injury detail: bruises, burns, broken bones, and physical trauma referenced in survival and combat scenes.

Kidnapping / detainment: characters captured, transported in vans, or detained by soldiers.

To the ones who believe that hope is the most powerful weapon of all.

CHAPTER 1

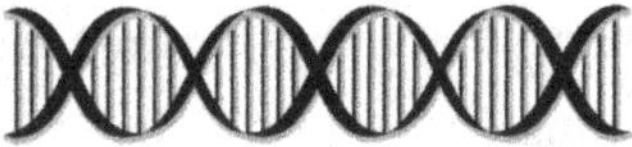

KYLE STEPS ONTO THE MATS, the world narrowing to the space between him and his opponent. He bounces on the balls of his feet, the hum of new energy vibrating through his muscles, whispering promises of victory. This is the last match of the day. The final. It all hinges on this moment.

His opponent stands opposite, a wall of muscle, sweat gleaming under the harsh arena lights. They circle. Kyle's pulse quickens. This is his first competition since taking the speed nanite.

The pill was delivered to him at a fancy catered dinner his Mom organized at home. Wrapped in a box with a ribbon. Speed isn't the obvious choice for karate, but Kyle wanted something different, something his opponents hadn't opted for, something that would give him an edge. There are no bulks in the karate circuit, yet. And Kyle didn't fancy being all jacked up and looking like he was juiced up on steroids, so speed it was. And it will give him an advantage against a bulk anyway.

He's spent the last week testing out his new limits. Grinning like a fool when he played out scenarios on EvolveMe. Smiling even harder when he took down opponents who didn't see him coming.

Claus, his sensei, has banned him from sparring with unadjusteds. Fair enough, Kyle reasons. Unadjusteds and altereds should never be pitted against each other. That's when things go wrong.

But now it's time to show the world what he's got. It's an important match. And he's the youngest person in the country to receive a Class 7 nanite. *Thanks Mom and Dad.* And also—no pressure.

He glances at Jax in the audience, his expression a complex mixture of admiration and determination. He's kitted out in the same dojo uniform as Kyle, but they won't be competing against each other. Jax hasn't taken a nanite. Yet.

Kyle notes the jealousy flickering through his best friend's eyes. Jax is taller, more muscular, maybe a better contender for a nanite. But Kyle got there first. On account of his dad being a spin doctor for the president and his mom being a nanite influencer with a gazillion followers. They didn't even have to pay for it.

He's lucky. He knows that. And if he could get Jax a nanite, he would. Hopefully his best friend will understand it's just a matter of time. Kyle has seen nanites tear more than one friendship apart. But that won't happen with him and Jax. They've known each other since kindergarten. Their moms are best friends. They're *bros*.

The referee signals. Kyle moves before the sound has fully left the whistle. His body reacts faster than thought, faster than instinct, faster than what should be humanly possible. *Sweet.* He launches toward his opponent, cursing himself for being too caught up in his own head just a moment ago, but that doesn't seem to matter now because he just dodged the first strike without trying.

He sidesteps a jab with such ease it feels like watching someone practice in slow motion, then counters with a flurry of strikes that connect before his opponent can blink. Each hit lands exactly where he wants it to, but it feels like he's beating up a practice dummy. This isn't skill alone anymore. This is something else. Something more. Something almost godly.

Kyle snaps his arm down in a fierce karate chop that smacks against his opponent's guard, the sound as sharp as the crack of splitting wood. The force drives his rival back a step, shock flashing across the boy's eyes, but he doesn't fall. Not yet.

His opponent lunges, muscles coiled like springs. To Kyle, it's laughable—every twitch of muscle, every bead of sweat flying from his brow happens at a crawl. Kyle weaves under a kick, grinning, a laugh bubbling up from his chest at the absurdity of it all.

This is so freaking cool!

He remembers when this boy used to beat him with his reflex nanites, back when Kyle's speed was human. Now, even enhanced reflexes look clumsy and predictable. The world stutters, dragging behind while Kyle races ahead.

The joy of it is undeniable. Each step, each dodge, each strike is a secret that belongs only to him. The crowd gasps, but Kyle hears it like a delayed echo, his body already moving on to the next motion, the next advantage. He could end the match at any moment, and the knowledge sends a thrill through him—tinged with a sliver of unease. If this is what one nanite can do, what happens when everyone takes one? What happens when speed isn't his gift anymore, but just another product in a bottle?

Then he catches her eye—Silver Melody, standing at the back of the bleachers. Her dark hair pulled into a messy knot, her silver eyes assessing. Her concern reaches him even from this distance.

His opponent scores a point against him. *Not cool.*

Kyle blinks, centers himself. *Focus,* he commands, thrusting away the internal debate. His opponent spins, an arc of fury aimed at Kyle's side. But Kyle is gone, moving with impossible speed, time bending around him. He strikes—a clean punch to the shoulder, sending his opponent spiraling down to the mats.

Something cracks, but the sound is covered by the erupting crowd. Noise floods his senses as medics rush toward the fallen rival, checking vitals, lifting him onto a stretcher. Kyle doesn't have the strength to hit someone hard enough to break a bone... but with added speed...? He never considered that possibility.

Crap.

Cheers wash over him in dizzying waves. Cameras flash. Smiles stretch.

Kyle pulls in a breath, finds his parents in the audience. They are beaming at him. Well, no, not at him. That's for the cameras. There are national network cameras here and his parents never miss an opportunity to increase their political reputation or follower counts. Since his mom got the turquoise eye-enhancing nanite, her following has doubled. It's become a family joke over the breakfast table when she logs on each morning to guess how many more she accrued overnight. Kyle always gets it wrong. Always underestimates. Never understands how many people love social media. Okay, yeah, he has his own following on EvolveME, but that's different. It's gaming. It's not jewelry and makeup and vacationing on an island.

Kyle leans down to his opponent before they wheel him away. He can't even remember his name. "Dude, I'm really sorry."

His opponent shrugs his good arm. "Don't worry about it. Nothing that a regen nanite won't fix."

The injured opponent is wheeled away. As well-wishers surround him, he's swept from the mats. He takes what feels like hours to fight his way through the crowds to the locker room, and by the time he gets there, he's exhausted.

The locker room is quieter than the arena, the echo of cheers replaced by the muffled hum of ventilation. Kyle sits on a bench, sweat cooling on his skin, hands still trembling with the aftershocks of speed. The adrenaline feels endless, like the nanite won't let him crash.

Claus finds him a couple of minutes later. He places a hand on Kyle's shoulder. "You fought well, Kyle-kun. *Yoku yatta.*" *Well done.* His mouth curves into the faintest smile. "I am proud."

Kyle lets out a shaky laugh, the sound bouncing around the tiled walls. "Thanks, Sensei. I mean, did you see that? I was untouchable out there. Everything felt so... easy. Like I could see his moves before he even thought them."

Claus' expression doesn't change. "That is the danger." His voice is low. "*Jōnetsu wa chikara ni naru, shikashi yami ni mo naru.*" *Passion can become strength, but it can also become darkness.* He squeezes Kyle's shoulder, firm enough to ground him. "You are fast, faster than any man has a right to be. But karate is not about speed. It is about control. And balance."

Kyle swallows, the words subduing the high of his win. "I had control. Didn't I?"

Claus' gaze flickers to the mats visible through the open door, where sweat and blood still stains the floor. "Your fist says otherwise. You did not mean to hurt him, but intent and consequence do not always walk the same path. Never forget that."

Kyle nods, but the energy in his veins makes stillness impossible. He wants to move, to run, to fight again. He forces himself to meet Claus' eyes. "I'll be careful, Sensei."

Claus' voice softens. "Do not lose your head. You are a good boy, Kyle." He gets to his feet. "Remember—without discipline, speed is nothing but chaos."

Claus leaves him in the locker room to shower. Kyle has no more time to debate his conflicting feelings; his parents are waiting to take him to dinner. He goes through the motions of washing his hair and scrubbing his body, trying to pretend he doesn't hear the echo of the crunch of his opponent's shoulder breaking. But that is what regen nanites are for. They fix what's broken. And if you're going to play competitive sport, things are going to get broken.

Outside, Kyle finds the family car waiting for him. Harris

is in the driver's seat, hands on the steering wheel, white hat perched neatly on his head. It's a driverless car, but his parents like the ceremony of a driver. Said parents are in the back, both their faces lit up by their phone screens. They're laughing and smiling at each other, sharing bytes from their socials. No doubt about Kyle's dramatic win.

Harris spots Kyle, comes out of the car, and opens the door for Kyle to climb in.

Kyle slides into the leather seat, the door clicking shut behind him. His mother barely glances up from her phone before beaming at him, turquoise eyes shining with artificial brilliance. "Darling, you were incredible. The angles, the power—perfect for the highlight reels. My followers are already trending the clip." She squeezes his hand once, then turns her screen so Kyle can see a loop of his karate chop slowed down to cinematic perfection. The caption reads: *The Future of Sport—Kyle Lewis.*

His father leans forward, voice brimming with approval. "You showed control, son. Precision. Exactly what the program needs to see. I've already had two calls from officials wanting a statement. Tonight, you'll be the face of progress. Remember that." He pats Kyle's shoulder.

The car pulls away, Harris guiding it smoothly through the neon-lit streets of Central City. Digital billboards flash by, some already updated with Kyle's image mid-strike, his name bold beneath the NanoTech insignia.

His mother's laughter bubbles again as she scrolls, tilting her screen toward his father. "The Helix Lounge posted— they're reserving the crystal chamber just for us." She turns to Kyle, pride radiating from every polished pore. "Everyone will be there tonight, sweetheart. Politicians, influencers, sponsors. And all of them will want to meet *you*."

Kyle's not sure how he feels about that, but he nods and smiles just like he's expected to.

The candlelight in The Helix Lounge flickers over the polished tables, illuminating fine china and silver utensils. Kyle sits opposite his parents, scanning the menu, wondering when food started costing so much. But apparently their meal is *on the house,* and they can order *anything they like.* Kyle barely recognizes any of the words on the menu and asks the waiter to bring him something "simple." He's secretly hoping for a burger, not a holoshrimp cocktail or gene bean tartlets.

Their glasses are filled to the brim with champagne. Even Kyle's despite the fact he's only twelve.

"I'm so proud of you, son." His dad raises his glass.

The three of them clink, but Kyle doesn't sip before placing the crystal flute on the table.

His mom smiles. "You'll learn to love it."

"Maybe when I'm older."

His dad laughs and ruffles his hair. Like old times.

Kyle ducks under his hand and scans the seated guests, hoping no one noticed his dad being so embarrassing.

As they wait for their starters, his mom pushes her phone across the table. "Look. Sponsors are already offering. They saw how easily you won today, Kyle. You are the future of karate—"

"I'm nothing like Jacob Shea—"

His dad waves a dismissive hand. "He's older than you and he's taken a lot more nanites."

"Exactly," his mom agrees. "And there's no reason you

can't surpass his standard. With the right training. The right nanites. The right backing—"

Kyle throws up both hands, almost knocking his plate from the waiter's grasp. He's disappointed to see shells and cabbage and other things he can't identify. It does not look simple. "I thought I was just getting the speed nanite. I didn't think..." *It was going to become a whole thing.*

Both his parents frown.

"You can't stop at one," his dad says.

"You have to fight hard to stay at the top," his mom says.

As the waiter lays their food in front of them, Kyle gives his parents a once-over. Apart from his mom's turquoise eyes, there's nothing obviously altered about them. But he knows they've both taken numerous nanites. Lesser ones that help them with their careers. Kyle gave up counting the packets that came through the doors a couple of years ago. At least they haven't opted for antlers or bunny tails. *Jeez.*

Not that he has anything against anyone who does choose those. Each to their own and all that. It's just not right for Kyle.

The waiter leaves.

"Anyway," his mom says, pointing at her phone. "There is more than one nanite to help you on the mat." She scrolls through endless streams of Class 6 and Class 7 nanite choices. The options start to blur in Kyle's head. Her murmurs rise over the din of the restaurant, discussing the merits of enhanced reflexes and teleportation, as if shopping for clothes.

"This could guarantee your future edge," she says, eyes not lifting from the list, food untouched.

His dad echoes her sentiment with his spin-doctor vocabulary. "We'll invest in anything that cements your lead."

Kyle nudges a shell with his fork. He thinks it's a snail. They're going through a French phase at The Helix Lounge. All he wants is a burger and a chocolate shake.

His thoughts tumble. His stomach growls. His parents urge him to dig in. The match plays in his mind, as well as the crack of breaking bone.

CHAPTER 2

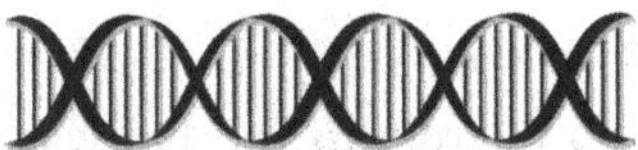

THE NANITE IS ONLY the start of it.

Despite his father being a prominent political figure and his mom a mega influencer, Kyle never expected it to change his life. Yeah, he'll win more competitions, maybe a national trophy—*sweet*—but all of the speeches and interviews and other crap that goes with it? It never stops.

But he can't complain. He wouldn't be winning if his parents weren't who they were. So he's not going to be ungrateful. He knows how privileged he is. He knows he's lucky.

"Hey, can I get a selfie, dude?" asks a fellow freshman, already moving in for the pose. Kyle looks for an escape, but the hallway is crowded and he finds himself wedged into the guy's side. A future linebacker in the making. A bulk nanite on the horizon.

"Sure." He smiles, pose perfected by repetition. The click of the camera feels almost like a rebuke, but he's not sure why. Maybe he's just tired. In spite of the stamina nanite his Mom made him swallow last month.

Ahead, Silver leans against a locker. Their eyes meet, and something passes between them—does she get what it feels like to be him? Kyle shakes his head. How could she? She's an unadjusted.

What is it like to be her?

Kyle turns a slow circle in the hallway. Sees the wings, the muscles, the speed, the horns... so many signs of altereds. In her eyes, it must look like a freaking zoo. To his, too.

His gaze falls to her cuff. Not just an unadjusted, but an unadjusted under house arrest. That sucks.

Avoiding any more selfies, Kyle makes his way into his classroom. Jax stands on a desk, addressing a dozen of their friends. His voice carries to the back of the room. He's always loved a dramatic moment.

"Enhancements are evolution. It's about becoming your best self," Jax declares, green eyes gleaming with passion. Jax got his speed nanite only a few weeks after Kyle. But he's never beaten Kyle in a race or on the mats. They've remained best friends, but there's an unmistakable edge to their friendship now.

Jax catches his eye, a brief connection.

By the time PE rolls around, the sun burns through the cloudless sky, and the track shimmers with heat. Coach lines them up, gruffly barking, "Three laps, let's see what you've got."

The whistle blows. Kyle explodes forward, legs pumping, body slicing through the air. He didn't mean to activate his speed, but nothing else burns through the restless energy that makes him permanently edgy. He glances back once, more out of habit than need. The others are dots, even Jax, his movements sharp but nowhere near fast enough to catch him.

By the time Kyle finishes, barely winded, the rest of the class is still rounding the second bend. He pulls up, grinning despite himself, sweat gleaming on his skin.

Jax crosses the line next, chest heaving, but his smile is wide. "Ladies and gentlemen, *Team Kyle*! The fastest legs this side of Central City!" He claps Kyle on the back, his laughter a shade too loud. "I swear, the guy doesn't even sweat anymore. Must be hiding an extra nanite in his sock."

A few students chuckle. Someone mutters, "Seriously, how is anyone supposed to compete with that?"

Jax raises his arms theatrically. "We don't compete—we *witness*! Kyle Lewis, record-smasher, law of physics-breaker, my best friend. We're lucky he even shows up to class."

The crowd laughs, and Kyle musters a smile. It's good-natured, sure, but behind the jokes, he hears what Jax isn't saying: *I should be the fastest.*

Kyle has no idea why the nanite has combined so well with his DNA. Although it's hard to get hold of a speed nanite as a teenager, he's not the only one, not by far. But he is the fastest. Which he proves time and time again. There's nothing quite like the thrill of a win, but when there's no real competition, it does start to get a bit repetitive.

Lunchtimes are weird. Two years ago, they all crammed around the same tables, swapping chips and stories, arguing over who got to play striker in the afternoon game. Now, the cafeteria is split down the middle. Altereds crowd one side, showing off new tricks—sparks dancing from fingertips, skin flashing like polished steel, laughter punctuated by the crack of someone accidentally denting a chair. In the corner, the unadjusteds cluster together, their voices edged with the bitterness of kids who know they're being left behind.

Kyle floats somewhere in the middle. His status demands he sit with the altereds, but sometimes he catches himself glancing toward the other side. He remembers what it felt like to belong without qualifiers, before nanites became the currency of popularity. Now, when he tries to cross the cafeteria to say hi to an old friend, conversations stall, eyes follow him, and the space he walks through feels like a gulf instead of a passageway.

Even in class, the split shows. Altereds dominate sports, theater, debate—anywhere speed, strength, or enhancements tilt the balance. The unadjusteds slip further into the shadows, grades and talents eclipsed by flashy abilities. Kyle notices teachers praise victories louder when a nanite is involved, as though hard work has lost its shine. He hates how natural it feels to accept it, especially when Silver's silver eyes burn with silent disapproval when she's flipped onto a mat.

The change is everywhere. Hallways filled with posters celebrating "The Future" that feature altered kids like him. School assemblies with guest speakers from NanoTech reminding them to "choose wisely." Even in his friend group, jokes have edges sharper than they used to. Jax hides envy behind a grin. Others hide fear behind silence.

As for himself, he keeps his head down, smiles for the cameras, and ducks under karate chops on the mats.

A few days later he finds himself outside his locker gathering books for the day when a strained voice grabs his attention. He turns to see Silver with two of her friends, Matt and Diana. He doesn't know them well, them being older and all, but he's well aware of Diana's talent in the pool. She's getting almost as much attention as Kyle.

Something is clearly eating her. Her face is pale and drawn. Then Kyle spots the nanite in her hand. He doesn't keep track of what other people take—none of his business—but because of her campaign and the way her parents are as pushy as his, Kyle knows this isn't her first. Or second. Or even third.

Matt hovers on Diana's other side, clutching a bundle of wires and scrap circuits like he can't bear to be seen without a project in his hands. They're talking fast, voices urgent even over the hallway noise.

Kyle slows his pace, fiddling with the strap of his backpack, pretending to retie his shoelace so he doesn't look like he's staring. But he is.

He watches the small pill in Diana's hand. Is she going to take it now?

Silver grabs Diana's hand, obviously pleading with her. But Diana just shakes her head and gives them a tight smile, the kind of smile Kyle's mom uses for the cameras—bright on the outside, hollow underneath.

She tips her head back. Swallows.

Kyle's breath sticks in his throat.

For a moment, nothing happens. The hallway buzzes as usual—kids laughing, scrolling through phones, rushing for homeroom. For a heartbeat, the world looks normal.

Then Diana staggers.

Her hand shoots to her throat. Her face twists, first in confusion, then in pain. She gasps, a raw sound that makes the hairs on Kyle's arms rise. Her knees buckle, books thudding to the floor.

Silver lunges forward, catching her before she hits the linoleum. Matt drops to his knees, fumbling for his phone.

The crowd hushes as if someone pressed mute.

Kyle's legs freeze. He wants to move, to help, but he can't. His body is built for speed, but right now he's slower than everyone. Slower than the horror unfolding before him.

Diana convulses. Foam bubbles at her lips. Her eyes widen, terrified, hands clawing at her neck as if she can rip the nanite back out. Silver cradles her head, tears streaking her face, murmuring something Kyle can't hear. Matt shouts into his phone, begging for help, his voice cracking.

The foam turns yellow. It gushes from Diana's mouth, her nose, even her ears. Her body thrashes, heels drumming against the floor. The sound is sickening.

Kyle flinches. His stomach lurches, bile rising in his throat.

Teachers burst out of classrooms, shouting for space. Students are shoved back against the lockers, pressed shoulder-to-shoulder, horrified and useless. No one wants to look, but no one can look away.

Kyle squeezes his fists until his nails dig into his palms. *Do something.* His mind screams it, but his body won't move. He's supposed to be fast, the fastest, yet he's rooted to the floor while Diana drowns in foam.

Silver's voice rises above the chaos, raw and desperate.

"You're not going to die! Do you hear me? You're not going to die!"

Diana's reply is strangled, broken. *I don't want to die.*

The words punch through Kyle's chest. He bites down hard, almost drawing blood. His parents told him nanites were safe. That accidents were rare. That anyone who didn't survive was weak, unfit. But Diana isn't weak. She's a champion. She's—

Her body jerks one final time. Bloody yellow foam streaks down her chin. Then she goes limp.

Silver lets out a sound that tears the hallway apart. She bends over her friend's body, rocking, sobbing, screaming at anyone who tries to get close. Matt slams his fists against the floor, his face twisted in fury and grief.

Kyle can't breathe. His chest is a cage, his heart battering against the bars.

The first bell rings. Shrill. Indifferent. Its piercing sound slices through the horror. Students jolt like they've been shocked, but no one moves.

Paramedics arrive, pushing through with gurneys and equipment. They kneel beside Diana, checking vitals, but it's too late. Everyone can see it. Everyone knows.

Silver won't let go. She wraps herself tighter around her friend, screaming at the medics, at her guard, at the universe. Her voice is hoarse. They have to pry her fingers loose.

Kyle stumbles back until his shoulder hits the cold metal of the stairwell railing, moving away from the terrible scene. He scrubs a hand across his face, but it comes away wet.

Someone grips his arm—maybe a teacher, maybe an official—and drags him toward homeroom. Their voice is just noise. He doesn't hear the words. All he hears is Diana's last plea.

I don't want to die.

✕✕✕✕✕

The next morning, the school is suffocatingly silent. No school should sound like this. Kyle walks around long after the bell rings. There is no sign of Silver or Matt. Of course not.

With a sigh, he walks to homeroom and slides into his seat.

The intercom crackles. The principal's voice comes through, careful and heavy. "Students, we gather today under very sad circumstances. Yesterday we lost one of our own. Diana was a beloved student, an extraordinary athlete, a friend to many. She will be deeply missed."

A murmur ripples through the classroom. Heads bow. Some kids wipe their eyes. Others stare at the floor.

Kyle doesn't move. His throat is tight, his hands clenched in his lap. The words feel wrong. Too neat. Too clean for what he saw. For the foam, the convulsions, the raw terror on Diana's face.

The announcement drones on, offering counseling services, encouraging students to reach out, but Kyle barely hears it.

The bell rings again, and students shuffle out quietly. Kyle stays seated, staring at his hands. *If this is the future, why does it feel like we're killing ourselves to get there?*

Kyle goes through the motions of school. He shouldn't

have come in. Everyone would understand. But there's a part of himself that feels… guilty. He's taken nanites. More than one. Maybe more than Diana. And he's never had a negative side-effect. How is that fair?

He walks for hours after school, avoiding home, avoiding his parents, avoiding questions, but he can't get out of his own head.

When he does eventually return home, the house oozes its usual luxury. His mother scrolls through her feeds, turquoise eyes flashing in the glow. "The coverage is tragic, of course, but respectful," she says, tapping a screen. "It was a rare side effect. Statistically insignificant."

His father doesn't look up from his drink. "The program can't afford fearmongering. Sacrifices will always be made for progress. Diana's death will be used to strengthen safety protocols." He finally lifts his gaze, pinning Kyle with a sharp look. "You understand that, don't you?"

Kyle swallows hard. He nods, because it's easier. Because arguing won't change anything.

But inside, something breaks.

He remembers Silver's scream. Matt's helpless fists. The foam staining the floor. Diana whispering that she didn't want to die.

He doesn't sleep that night. He lies in the dark, staring at the ceiling, the words pounding in his head.

I don't want to die.

CHAPTER 3

A FEW MONTHS LATER, Kyle finds Silver in the gym in her training gear. She's a couple of belts ahead of him, even though she's only an unadjusted, and that's damn impressive. He'd love to fight her, but that wouldn't be fair. But damn, she's amazing to watch. Every jab is considered. Every kick well-intentioned. Every muscle honed to perfection. It's hard to believe she hasn't taken a nanite. But maybe it's the cuff that gives her that extra determination.

Hell, if his mom had been arrested and thrown in jail, if his dad was President Bear's lapdog... oh wait, he kind of is.

The realization slams into Kyle with more strength than a bulk fist. He's been played. Manipulated. In a world where he never had any choice. But he knew that, didn't he? In some ways, he's fighting the same things Silver is. But he hasn't got a clue how to go about it. How can one person change anything?

"Are you joining us, Kyle?" Claus calls, standing at the edge of the mat, his eyes on Silver as she performs a Kata.

Kyle nods, tightening his belt and stepping barefoot onto the mats. The air smells faintly of sweat and polish, grounding him in a way press conferences never can. He bows, then takes his place beside Silver.

They begin the sequence together. Silver moves so fluidly Kyle can barely take his eyes off her. She makes Kyle look like an awkward duckling. Her fists snap out in sharp strikes, her stances are rooted with conviction. Kyle mirrors her motions, but his speed feels wrong here. Too much, too quick. The Kata isn't about how fast you can be. It's about discipline, breath, and unity of body and mind. Watching Silver, he realizes she doesn't need speed. She is control personified.

Her sidekick slices the air, clean and powerful. Kyle throws his own, faster, but he knows it lacks intention. He sneaks a glance at her—sweat darkening her hairline, eyes sharp as steel. She owns every move.

Kyle's chest tightens. This is what they're all forgetting. Not the nanites, not the propaganda, not the endless "future of progress" speeches. *This.* The grit. The repetition. The mastery. Silver proves with every strike that skill doesn't need enhancement, only discipline.

As they finish the Kata with a final unified block, Kyle lowers his arms. For the first time in years, pride burns in his chest without being tangled up in NanoTech slogans. He admires her, truly admires her. And in that admiration comes a seed of clarity: maybe the system is wrong. Maybe faster, stronger, altered isn't better. Maybe the divide being shoved down their throats isn't about progress at all.

Claus claps once, nodding in approval. "Good. *Yoku dekita.*" Well done. His eyes rest on Kyle, searching, as if his sensei knows he's wrestling with something much heavier than form.

Kyle bows, his gaze flicking to Silver. They sit on a bench together sipping water from flasks, watching the other students perform Katas.

"What's it like?" Silver asks, not taking her eyes from the students on the mats. "Having all that power, with everyone watching you?"

Kyle fiddles with the end of his brown belt. No one has asked him that before. He suddenly feels naked. Exposed. Found wanting. "It's... a lot," he admits. "The speed, it's like being free and trapped at the same time. Everyone wants something. And I don't always know what that is. Or if I should give it."

He's never told anyone that. His parents would kill him. Probably literally. But there's something about Silver he trusts. She is an unadjusted after all. Or does she think he's just another privileged alt?

Her gaze softens, her silver eyes inviting him in. "What do you think it's like for us? Those who can't afford the pills, or who don't want them?"

Kyle pulls his lip between his teeth, gives it a chew. He lets out a sigh. "To be honest, I've been thinking a lot about that lately. And it's not my place to imagine—"

"Cut the bullcrap."

He startles, then laughs when he sees she's smiling.

"Dude, I can't imagine," he says. "I was born with opportunities."

"So was I."

"And I took all of them handed to me."

She tilts her head. "I suppose I could have too."

"But you didn't." He says it like she's the one who made the right decision.

"I had my reasons."

"So did I." Truth. How could he have *not* taken a nanite with the parents he has? And yet, Silver's parents invented the nanite pill. How had *she* not taken one? "I didn't think it would be like this."

She leans closer. "What did you think it would be like?"

Kyle blushes, aware that he's two years younger and so much more immature. So much more unaware. So much more... everything. "I just wanted to win fights."

She laughs. The sound somehow soothes his soul.

Silver grips his knee, squeezes, and he finds himself laughing right along with her, but he's not sure what's so funny.

"You're a good kid, Kyle."

"I like to think so?"

She smiles. "You are."

After practice, Kyle pulls on his hoodie and slings his bag over his shoulder, the words *you're a good kid* echoing in his head louder than the shuffle of his sneakers against the pavement. *Good kid.* He wants to believe her.

The streets are alive with after-school energy. Clusters of kids spill from the gates, some flaunting their enhancements —sparks crackling across knuckles, bursts of speed carrying them across crosswalks, wings unfurling in flashes of color. Their laughter is sharp, cocky, arrogant.

Then Kyle sees them. Three unadjusted kids, younger than him, pressed against the chain-link fence while a bulk shoves them, mocking their *slow reflexes* and *weak arms*. Another alt sneers, wagging glowing fingers just inches from one boy's face. The unadjusteds try to joke back, but the fear in their eyes is obvious.

Kyle stops in the middle of the sidewalk. Once, he might have laughed along or walked past, pretending it wasn't his problem. But after Silver's words, after watching her fight with nothing but grit, the sight knots something inside him. This isn't banter. This is the beginning of the end.

He clenches his fists. The speed thrums in his veins, begging to be unleashed, whispering that he could end this in a blink. And then he moves.

In a flash he's between the bulk and the smallest unadjusted kid, his voice more confident than he feels. "That's enough."

The bulk sneers at him, recognition flickering in his eyes. "Well, if it isn't Central City's golden boy. What's the matter, Lewis? Don't want us reminding these losers of their place?"

Kyle doesn't flinch. "Their place is the same as yours. On the mat. On the track. In school. They don't owe you respect just because you popped a pill."

A few of the onlookers mutter, shifting uneasily. The unadjusteds behind him straighten a little.

The bulk cracks his knuckles, a low laugh rumbling in his chest. "You think you can stop me?"

Kyle feels the nanite singing in his veins. But he doesn't need to show off. He doesn't need to fight. He takes a single step forward, too fast for the eye to track, and suddenly he's nose-to-nose with the boy. "Try me."

The bulk falters, just for a moment. Then he scoffs and

backs away, covering his hesitation with bravado. "Whatever, man. Not worth my time." He motions to his friends, and they peel off, leaving the fence rattling in their wake.

Kyle exhales, tension draining from his body. He turns to the unadjusteds, offering a small smile. "You okay?"

They nod, wide-eyed. One of them whispers, "Thanks, Kyle."

Kyle wants to say something else, but he's not sure what that thing is. But there is one important thing he has realized: if he doesn't use what he's been given to make a stand, then he really *is* just the poster boy they want him to be.

But, how exactly, does he go about making a stand?

)()()()(

Two years speed by, every day marked by the same cycle of appearances and obligations. Press events multiply until they merge together, their locations indistinguishable—conference halls, sports arenas, glitzy rooftops. The cameras always flash the same, the microphones always thrust forward with the same hungry questions. *How does it feel to be the fastest? What's next for Central City's rising star?*

He smiles on cue, delivers the lines he's rehearsed until they're etched into muscle memory. His answers are pre-packaged sound bites stitched together by his father's careful coaching. "The nanites have opened a new world of possibilities for me," he states again and again, each time convincing the crowd, but never quite convincing himself. Even though it's true.

His dad nods approvingly from the sidelines. For the

cameras, his father is the proud statesman, the guiding hand behind his son's meteoric rise. For Kyle, that nod has become a leash. He longs for the simplicity of running just because he loved the wind in his face, the feeling of freedom with each stride. That joy has been rewritten into responsibility.

At the dojo, Kyle finds a fleeting reprieve. Here, when the mats are beneath his feet, he lets his body move on instinct, strikes landing wherever he wants them to. The air shivers with each blur of his fists and kicks. For a heartbeat, he feels free. But even the dojo becomes another stage. Word of his abilities spread, and soon spectators fill the observation benches. Journalists sneak in, eager for glimpses of "the fastest boy alive." The sanctuary where he once tested his limits becomes another theater, the echoes of his training drowned by the clatter of applause. Until Claus puts a stop to it. And even though his parents protest, Claus doesn't back down. Kyle can breathe again. It is his one safe place where he can be himself. Whatever that is now. He's not sure he knows anymore.

In the afternoons, his schedule shifts to exhibitions at local elementary schools. It becomes part of his brand: Kyle Lewis, racing through playgrounds while children watch with wide-eyed awe. He jogs onto cracked asphalt and grass fields, waves at the sea of eager faces, then explodes into motion. Gasps follow him as he streaks past, circling their jungle gyms and swing sets in less than a breath. He stops beside them, grinning despite the fatigue gnawing at his bones. "Again, again!" they plead, their voices bubbling with wonder. He obliges, time after time, each lap peeling away another sliver of his sense of self. If he's exhausted, no one notices. If he's unhappy, no one asks. All they see is speed. All they want is more.

He is tipped to be the next Jacob Shea. Kyle has no idea how to feel about that. He wonders if Jacob hates all the attention too.

When night falls, and the city lights dim, Kyle lies awake in bed. His body screams for rest, but his mind refuses to silence. Questions linger like shadows. Is he running toward his future or away from who he used to be? Who *did* he used to be, exactly?

One night at dinner, Kyle finally lets the words slip out between the solar-grilled skyfish and the Veloskin duck breast. Food he's never heard of. "Mom, Dad... what if I don't want to keep doing all the appearances? What if I just... want to compete for myself again?"

His mother's fork pauses in midair, turquoise eyes narrowing. "Kyle, darling, you *are* competing for yourself. Don't you see? Every appearance, every camera flash, every headline—it's proof of your greatness. People *need* to see you."

His father leans forward, steepling his fingers under his chin. "Son, we've worked hard to put you where you are. This isn't just about you anymore. It's about legacy. About what you represent to the country. You can't throw that away."

"We can get you an Enduro nanite, if you're tired," his mom says, completely missing the point.

"I'm not saying I want to quit," Kyle mutters, heat rising in his cheeks. "I just... sometimes I don't feel like me out there. Like I'm somebody else's idea of who I should be."

His father's expression hardens. "Then get used to it. That's what greatness feels like."

Greatness? Kyle thinks of the Jacob Shea digi-posters hanging on the walls of his bedroom. Is that what greatness feels like for him too?

His mother smiles tightly, already turning her attention back to the solar-grilled skyfish. "Don't worry, sweetheart. It will all be worth it. I promise."

Kyle sinks back in his chair. Thinks of all the unadjusteds he knows. How they seem to be managing just fine. Okay, not fine *exactly*. It's not like they can compete in the same sports leagues... or even the academic ones... okay, maybe they don't have it so fine. But what is he supposed to do about it?

CHAPTER 4

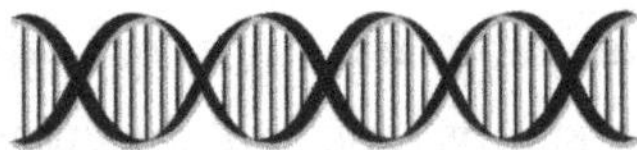

It's 2am.

Kyle stares at his ceiling, watching shadows stretch and dance across the plaster. Sleep refuses to come. His body vibrates with that familiar hum, low-level energy singing through his veins.

Jacob Shea digi-posters stare down at him from the walls, the world's most successful martial artist, smiling that million-dollar smile. Does he sit alone at night, wondering who he'd be without the pills?

Abandoning the idea of sleep, Kyle grabs his laptop and flicks it on.

He takes a breath, then logs into the dark web. He knows how. He's been here before. But his reason this time is completely different. His fingers blur across the keys, leaving ghost images in their wake.

"Come on, baby. Be good to me," he whispers as he scrolls through website after website.

His heart hammers against his ribs. This is illegal.

Beyond illegal. This is the kind of thing that makes people disappear. He knows the rumors about black vans and midnight arrests, about people who ask too many questions vanishing from their homes. But he can't stop now.

A drip of sweat slides down his temple. He wipes it away, eyes never leaving the screen.

The first forum appears innocuous—discussion boards about nanite regulations and enhancement policies. But beneath the surface conversations, Kyle finds threads of coded language, usernames that hint at something deeper. Something hidden.

He clicks a link disguised as a technical manual. The page transforms, revealing a network of encrypted channels. Forums filled with words like "resistance" and "freedom fighters" and "unadjusted rights." His breath catches in his throat.

Holy shit.

He didn't know if this would exist. But of course it does. How can it not?

Minutes go by, then hours, as he reads, absorbing testimonials from parents who lost children to mandatory enhancement programs, scientists speaking out against the evolutionary dead-end of artificial advancement, stories of unadjusteds denied education and employment.

Kyle's fingers freeze above the keyboard. A name jumps out at him: Dr. Margaret Melody.

Silver's mother.

The post details her imprisonment, claiming she was arrested not for treason, but for developing a failsafe—a way to reverse nanite effects if needed. For advocating choice.

His eyes widen, pulse quickening. This contradicts everything his father has told him about the Melody case. About why Silver wears that cuff. About why her father never leaves his apartment building.

Kyle swallows, scanning faster, wishing his brain would work as fast as his feet. He finds mentions of underground meetings, safe houses where altereds and unadjusteds gather. Places where people question President Bear's vision of a "perfect future."

A notification pops up—someone's noticed his presence in the system. He receives a direct message.

"New here? Careful where you step."

Kyle hesitates. This is the moment to back out, to shut down his computer and pretend he never saw any of this. To go back to being the poster boy, the speed champion, his parents' perfect son.

Instead, his fingers fly: "Looking for truth."

Three dots pulse on screen. Then: " The truth is danger- ous. Are you ready to be altered?"

Kyle notes the play on words, feels in his heart he's in the right place. "Yes."

A link appears, giving him only a few seconds to copy it before it vanishes. It takes him to an web address. A password dings in his DMs seconds later.

He creates a profile—anonymous, untraceable. No mention of his speed, his fame, his family's connections to the administration. Just another curious mind seeking answers in a world that offers only carefully crafted lies.

The warehouse district. Tomorrow night. It could be a trap. He's risking everything. If he's caught, there will be no coming back from this betrayal.

But he also knows he can't unsee what he's seen. Can't unhear the whispers he's been listening to for years. Can no longer deny Diana's death. This divide isn't natural. The system isn't just.

Kyle closes his laptop, plunging his room back into darkness. For the first time in years, he feels like he has a purpose.

The next day, Kyle downs copious cups of coffee and twitches his way through school, counting down the hours and minutes until the secret meeting.

He shovels dinner into his mouth—some kind of OmegaStack steak his parents think has a high iron source—not speaking a word, muttering and nodding in all the right places so his parents won't suspect anything. Then he tells them he's taken on an extracurricular and is teaching younger kids about speed nanites. They beam at him.

Kyle leaves the house, runs through the streets so fast no security camera will be able to pick him up. He laughs at that. His ability working in his favor. How ironic.

The warehouse looms ahead, a hulking shadow against the midnight sky. He stops fifty yards away, scanning for surveillance drones, for unmarked vehicles, for any sign this is a setup. Broken windows are jagged teeth in a frozen mouth, rust creeps down metal walls like blood, and a single door hangs half-open like an invitation. Or a trap.

His breath forms small clouds in the cool air. The warehouse sits at the edge of the industrial district, abandoned when manufacturing moved overseas. Perfect for secrets. Perfect for revolution.

He approaches slowly.

The graffiti stops him cold. A symbol he's seen before. On

the website last night. He didn't think much of it at the time, but now he knows he's in the right place. The image is of a DNA helix split in half. With a bold line through it. The implication is obvious. *No altereds allowed.*

Kyle's hand unconsciously rises to touch his chest, as if the words could sense the enhancement in his blood. As if he could be rejected before he even enters.

But he's come too far to turn back.

He slips through the door, staying close to the wall. The interior smells of rust and damp concrete and too many bodies in too little space. Dim moonlight filters through broken skylights, supplemented by portable lamps positioned around what was once a loading bay. About twenty people sit on crates, folding chairs, and makeshift benches arranged in a rough semicircle.

As Kyle takes it all in, he catalogs details that send shock-waves through him.

A woman with delicate butterfly wings folded against her spine talks quietly with an unadjusted man. Three teenagers —one with metallic skin, two without any visible enhance-ments—huddle over a tablet, pointing and whispering. An elderly man with no apparent modifications cleans what looks like a taser.

Altereds and unadjusteds, sitting together. *Working* together. The sight alone contradicts everything Kyle has been told about the divide being natural, inevitable, necessary.

Then he sees her, and his blood freezes.

Mrs. Montoya. His Social Studies teacher. The one who taught them about the American Constitution, about civil liberties and the right to self-determination. The one who asked uncomfortable questions about historical parallels to the enhancement program.

She stands at the front of the gathering, her dark hair pulled into that familiar neat chignon, her sharp cheekbones accentuated by the harsh shadows. But instead of her usual professional attire, she wears a black shirt and black jeans.

"—surveillance has increased in sectors three and five," she's saying, her voice carrying the same authority it does in class, but with an edge Kyle has never heard before. "They're using enhanced drones with thermal imaging that can detect gathering patterns. We need to be more careful about our arrival and departure times."

Kyle presses deeper into the shadows, watching as a guy only a couple years older manipulates data on a tablet connected to a makeshift projection system. The holograms show city maps, security routes, scheduled drone sweeps. This isn't just people voicing complaints. This is a serious operation.

Kyle squints. The guy looks familiar—tall, sandy hair, intense concentration. Then it clicks. Matt Lawson. Silver's best friend.

"Intelligence says Dr. Melody might be at the Northwest Detention Center," Matt says, his voice tight with emotion. "She's still alive, but security is tight. They're keeping her isolated from other prisoners."

The name sends a ripple through the gathered group. Someone whispers, "Silver's mother," and Kyle's ears pick it up from across the room.

"What about Rufus?" asks a woman with scaled skin. "Is he still working for them?"

Mrs. Montoya—no, Francesca, they call her here—exchanges a glance with Matt. "Our sources say Dr. Melody is at the lab, but he's operating under heavy surveillance. The cuff on Silver's ankle isn't just for show. It's leverage."

"I heard he's developing something," says a man near the front. "A counter-nanite. Something that could neutralize enhancements."

"Or reverse them," adds another.

Kyle's pulse picks up. Reverse enhancements? Is that even possible? The implications thunder through his mind. His speed isn't just part of him—it's become his identity, his future, his currency in the world. The thought of losing it is terrifying.

And yet...

"Nothing is confirmed," Matt says firmly. "What matters is that Dr. Melody is being forced to develop more aggressive nanite technology against his will. And we know President Bear is set to make an announcement about an enforced program. Mandatory enhancements are coming. Choice is being eliminated."

Kyle scans the warehouse interior, noting security measures that would be invisible to most—signal jammers disguised as broken equipment, motion sensors hidden in debris piles, lookouts positioned near exits. These people aren't amateurs. They're organized, prepared, serious.

And yet, he slipped in. But then he does have speed on his side.

The meeting continues, discussions of safe houses for

unadjusteds fleeing enhancement mandates, underground channels for scientists who refuse to participate in the program, strategies for disrupting propaganda broadcasts. With each passing minute, Kyle absorbs more information that contradicts the polished narrative his father helps craft for the administration.

These aren't terrorists or luddites afraid of progress. They're people fighting for choice. For autonomy. For the right to remain human as they define it, not as President Bear decrees.

A chill runs through him. His father sits at meetings where these people are labeled enemies of the state. His mother's influence network promotes nanites as the only path to a better future. And here he stands, their son, their greatest success story, listening to the resistance with growing conviction that they might be right.

"New face," someone murmurs behind him, and Kyle turns to find himself staring into the suspicious eyes of a man with a jagged scar running from temple to jaw. "You vouched for?"

Kyle's throat dries up. He came prepared with a cover story—high school student, interested in resistance philosophy, no enhancements—but the lie sticks to his tongue. Before he can respond, a hand claps his shoulder.

"He's with me," says a familiar voice, and Kyle turns to find Matt standing beside him, expression unreadable. "Let's talk outside."

Kyle follows, heart thundering, wondering if he's just been made. If his double life is about to collapse around him.

They step into the alley's cold air. The door thunks shut

behind them, dulling the warehouse murmur. A sodium lamp sputters overhead, throwing light across cracked concrete and the oily shimmer of a puddle.

Matt doesn't say anything at first. He studies Kyle for a full minute. Up close, he looks older than he does at school—edges sharper, shoulders hunched with too many nights like this one.

"You shouldn't be here," Matt says finally.

Kyle swallows. "I think I should."

"You think," Matt echoes, mouth tilting. "That's new for your side of the posters."

Heat climbs Kyle's neck. "You don't know my side."

"I know the cameras," Matt says, quiet. "I know the sound bites. I know your dad writes some of them." He lifts his chin at Kyle's chest. "You wired?"

"No."

"Phone?"

"Off. Battery out. In a tin on my desk."

Matt's gaze flicks to Kyle's hands, to his sleeves, to his shoes. "Anklet?"

"I'm not cuffed."

"I know you have speed, anything else?"

Kyle hesitates. The lie would be easy. But truth is the only thing that matters out here.

"Increased reflexes and stamina." He rubs the back of his neck, trying to scratch the uncomfortable itch away. "Increased recovery time and enhanced processing skills. Oh, and EverFresh."

Matt chuckles, nods at the warehouse. "Everyone in there could do with one of those."

Kyle allows himself a small smile. "I came to listen."

"To what?" Matt asks.

Kyle holds strong. "To what's important."

"Why?" Matt leans one shoulder against the wall.

"Your friend... Diana." He looks away. That's not his grief to carry, but he does all the same.

Matt looks surprised. "You knew her?"

Kyle lifts a shoulder. "I saw her die."

"I didn't know you were there."

They stare at each other, some of the tension easing.

"Why did you wait so long to find us?" Matt asks.

"I didn't know you existed."

"Started the day Diana died."

Kyle's brows hitch up. "You started the resistance?"

Matt nods. "Along with Francesca and your sensei."

Holy shit. Sensei Claus?

"You want in?" Matt's eyes don't blink.

"I do," he says. And it's as simple as that.

Matt's mouth tightens. He looks toward the heart of the city. "You being here puts a target on us."

"I know."

"You don't. Not yet. Your last name unlocks doors and opens mouths. It also unlocks warrants." He pushes off the wall. "Why are you really here, Kyle? You like a girl?" His voice softens, kind and cruel at the same time.

Kyle shakes his head. "Nothing like that. I'm here because of Diana. And because of those kids at the fence. And because Claus looked at me and said speed without discipline is chaos and I realized I've been selling chaos with a smile."

Matt's posture shifts a millimeter.

"I'm here," Kyle says, "because every time my dad says *legacy*, someone who can't afford a pill gets dropped from AP classes or demoted from sports teams." He drags a hand through his hair, fingers shaking. "Because my mother posts about *empowerment* and all I can see is Silver's cuff."

The river burps; somewhere a barge groans. The warehouse breathes behind them—chair legs scrape, a voice rises, falls, the soft clack of a computer closing.

"You're still a risk," Matt says.

"I know," Kyle says again. "But I can be useful."

"How?" Matt asks. "Because you're fast? We don't need a mascot who outruns drones. We need people who know when *not* to move."

Kyle thinks of Claus' hands shaping air into form. "I can move slow," he says. "Claus is training me to." He hears the arrogance in it and swallows it back. "I mean—I'm learning. I can teach, too. Basics. Balance. How not to get broken by a bulk who thinks having armored skin means he owns the hallway."

Matt's mouth almost smiles. Almost. "Claus knows you're here?"

"Of course not." Kyle almost crosses his heart. "I haven't told a soul."

"Your presence will certainly give him a surprise."

Kyle tilts his head. "Or maybe not."

Matt taps his knuckles lightly against the wall. "What about your parents? They'll notice you slipping out."

"I'm... good at slipping."

"That's not a plan."

"It's a start."

The wind picks up, shivering the lamplight. Matt studies him. "You'll be asked to choose between the room with cameras and the room with risk," he says. "And you won't get to pick both. Not forever."

"I know," Kyle says softly.

Matt's eyes flick over Kyle's face. "If Rufus—if someone—builds a reversal protocol, you'd be willing to give it all up?"

"I don't know," he admits. "I like the feeling of being fast. I hate the feeling of being owned."

"Then don't be owned," Matt says simply. "Speed is not loyalty. It's a tool. Decide who gets to borrow it."

They stand in the hum of the city for a beat. A drone passes somewhere above the roofs—too far to matter.

Matt shifts his weight.

"Okay. Here are the rules if you want to help and not hurt. You show up when you say you will, and when you can't, you don't give a reason anyone can repeat. You don't bring tech we haven't blessed. You don't chase the word *cure* like it's a comet. You don't post anything that makes you feel righteous. And you learn to be bored while doing good, because most of this is sweeping floors and carrying crates and teaching someone where to put their feet."

Kyle nods after each sentence, relief and fear tightening in his chest. "Okay."

"And when your father asks you to stand behind a podium," Matt says quietly, "you slip in the word *choice*. You keep saying it. You smuggle that word into places I can't get it. You make it sound boring and reasonable, not radical."

"I can do that," Kyle says. He already has. He will again.

Matt pushes off the wall, offers an open palm. "One more thing," he says. "If I ever think you're endangering Silver, or anyone else, I cut you out. No speeches. No second chances."

"That's fair," Kyle says. He takes the offered hand.

Matt's grip is firm, warmer than Kyle expects.

"Welcome to the boring part," Matt says, letting go. "Francesca's going to assign you to logistics. Claus can use you on the mats after we clear the room. And I want you shadowing me for fifteen minutes tonight to learn how to get into this place—"

Kyle frowns. "But I just walked in and listened for fifteen minutes and no one knew I was there."

Matt chuckles. "Oh, I knew you were there. Had a drone on you from a mile out."

Kyle's mouth drops open.

Matt winks. "Wanted to see what you'd do."

CHAPTER 5

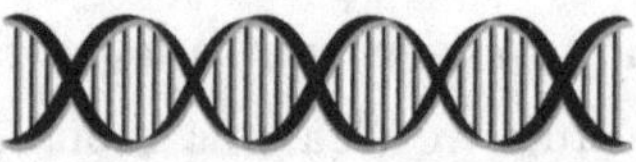

THE WAREHOUSE FEELS DIFFERENT TONIGHT. Less like a hiding place, more like a base of operations. Kyle slips through the side entrance, hood down. He's been coming for two weeks now, no longer a stranger but not yet trusted by all. Not surprising, considering his obvious celebrity.

The central floor has been cleared, mats laid out in a pattern he recognizes instantly from years of training. Bodies move in coordinated drills, unadjusteds and altereds side by side, learning to fight, to defend, to survive. And at the center of it all stands a figure Kyle would recognize anywhere—tall, gray-haired, mustached, with the ramrod posture that has corrected Kyle's stance a thousand times.

Sensei Claus.

Kyle freezes, instinctively stepping back into shadows. But it's too late—Claus' eyes find him and he smiles. Claus never smiles.

"We have a new volunteer," Claus announces, his

German accent carrying across the warehouse floor. He beckons with two fingers. "Kyle-kun. Join us."

Every head turns. Kyle feels exposed, pinned by two dozen stares that range from curious to hostile. He steps forward, conscious of his branded workout clothes, the expensive running shoes, all the trappings of his other life.

Claus waits until Kyle stands beside him, then addresses the group. "Today we learn how to defend against enhanced speed. Against opponents who move faster than the eye can track." He places a hand on Kyle's shoulder. "Kyle will demonstrate."

A murmur runs through the gathering. Kyle's heartbeat accelerates.

"I won't hurt anyone," he says quickly.

Claus' blue eyes find his. "That is not why you are here. You are here to teach them how *not* to be hurt."

Understanding dawns. Kyle nods. This he can do.

A volunteer steps forward—a woman in her twenties, no visible enhancements, determination etched in the set of her jaw. Kyle recognizes her from previous meetings. She works in a processing center and was recently demoted for refusing a nanite.

"Attack me," she says, taking a defensive stance.

Kyle hesitates. "At full speed?"

"At whatever speed you would use if you meant it."

Kyle glances at Claus, who nods once. Permission granted.

Kyle moves. The world blurs. He's behind the woman in less than a heartbeat, tapping her shoulder before she can react. She gasps, spinning too late. The crowd murmurs. Not the good kind. The scared kind.

"Again," Claus commands. "But this time, Lucy, remember what I taught you. Feel the air change. React not to what you see, but to what you sense."

Kyle circles, then attacks again, moving with enhanced speed toward the woman's blindside. But this time, as he approaches, she drops and pivots, using the floor as leverage. Kyle's momentum carries him forward, over her lowered shoulder. He catches himself before falling, but the point is made.

"Good," Claus says. "The enhanced rely on their gifts. They expect advantage. When you take that expectation and use it against them, you create opportunity."

For the next hour, Kyle works with different partners, demonstrating how his speed can be countered by anticipation, by the environment, by understanding that every enhancement comes with a weakness.

He doesn't feel quite so special anymore. He laughs at that. Hadn't realized he'd been holding on to his ego. *Special* can go fuck itself.

The unadjusteds move with a focus and precision that reminds him of Silver on the mats—no nanite-fueled power, just disciplined intention.

One partner, a stocky man with calloused hands, manages to trap Kyle in a hold despite his speed.

"How did you do that?" Kyle asks.

The man grins. "I've been wrestlin' bulks in the factory for years. Speed's fancy, but it still follows rules. Physics don't care how many nanites you swallowed."

Kyle laughs. The first genuine laugh he's experienced in months.

As the session winds down, participants disperse to various corners of the warehouse, some checking security feeds, others swapping stories, a few huddled around maps. Kyle helps roll up the mats, acutely aware he's being watched.

He turns to find Francesca studying him, arms crossed. "I'm proud of you," she says.

And dammit, his chest swells with pride. "I should have joined a long time ago. I should never have taken a nanite."

Francesca shakes her head. "Your experience has led you here. Not all gifts are bad. It's what you do with them that matters."

Her words resonate, and Kyle finally lets go of guilt.

"I am surprised you're here, with your parents doing what they do."

"I've seen some stuff."

She raises an eyebrow.

"Witnessed a nanite death." He swallows, memories surfacing.

"I'm sorry."

"My parents told me it was an isolated incident. That the program had been perfected since then. But I've watched how they treat Silver, how they treat all unadjusteds. Like they're..." He searches for the word. "*Inconvenient*. And I started wondering what else they're not telling me."

"He's one of the good ones," Matt says. "Silver talks about him. Says he's different from the others."

Kyle's head snaps up. "Silver talks about me?"

A ghost of a smile crosses Matt's face. "She says you see things others miss. That you ask questions when everyone else just accepts."

Something warm unfurls in Kyle's chest at the thought of Silver defending him.

As he leaves the warehouse, slipping back into the night, Kyle feels the double life solidifying around him. By day, the poster boy for progress. By night, a resistance fighter learning to dismantle the very system that made him. The contradiction should tear him apart, but instead, for the first time since taking the nanite, he feels whole.

✕✕✕✕✕

The forest is a wall. Interlocking trunks like prison bars. Kyle weaves through it.

He skips over rotting leaves and moss. But he's not stupid. Even with speed, the woods are treacherous. If you don't break an ankle, you'll run face-first into a startled deer and lose your teeth.

The hideout is out here. He just has to find it. Every resistance movement needs a safe house, and in this world, that means off grid. No drones, no sensors, no signal.

He vaults a log, dodges a thorned bush, and punches through a stand of saplings with enough force to rip a sleeve. His skin sizzles with scratches.

God, he missed this. Trees. Nature. Life. Unmodified.

A rabbit explodes from the brush ahead. Kyle locks eyes with it for a single, shared heartbeat. Then it vanishes in a blur of white.

It's been two days since he left Central City. Two days of sprints, forced catnaps, dehydrated food bars that taste like cardboard and chalk. But he wouldn't change a single second. The resistance is relying on him. Which should make him feel all the pressure in the world, but it only makes him grin.

The next morning, the ground is rimmed with dew. He doesn't slow down, despite skidding over wet mulch more than once. By noon, he's hit the marker—an ancient, moss-eaten stump, hollowed out by fire, the inside black and slick as pitch.

He circles the stump three times, just like the instructions said. He's supposed to follow the creek now, but the forest doesn't want to give up its secrets. He spends an hour looking for it. The stream is little more than a trickle, hidden under layers of dead leaves and last year's snow melt. He follows it, hands and knees, clothes catching on every hidden hook.

This is the last marker. This is as far as the resistance scouts have come. Kyle runs on. For two more freaking days. Feet kicking pinecones, breath coming in ragged bursts. He crests a ridge, windmills his arms so he doesn't tumble down the valley slope. It's a wide valley, with several copses of trees dotted around. His heart drops. There's so much land to explore. But that should make it hard for anyone to find them.

After glugging a few sips of water, Kyle makes his way down the valley at a slower pace, eyes to sky as he checks for drones and aircraft. He approaches the first clump of pine trees, sees how closely packed together they are and almost runs out of motivation.

Then he hears Diana's voice urging him on. He pictures Matt and Claus and Francesca's faces. They are relying on him. He is the only one with a speed nanite in the resistance. He can cover the most ground.

He pushes his way into the thick of it. Pines grow tight together, needle-to-needle, like they're conspiring. Light filters through in toxic green columns.

He reaches an area so thick he can go no further. Fauna clings to his calves. There is no wind. No birds. Just Kyle. On his own. Wishing he weren't. Dude, what he wouldn't give to have a buddy with him right now.

Just as he's about to turn back, something about the thickness of the darkness catches his eye. It doesn't look natural. He shifts his weight. The ground dips under his feet, spongy and uncertain.

Then he sees it.

Through the trunks, there's a seam—a vertical slit in the landscape, perfectly black.

His heart jumps.

He glances over his shoulder, just in case. Nothing. Not even a squirrel. He steps to the seam, brushes aside the curtain of vines and lichen. The opening is just wide enough.

Inside, the darkness is total. He clicks on his flashlight— the narrow beam cuts through a sudden, swirling mist. Air sucks at his face, hungry, ancient. It smells of salt and damp and secrets.

Emerging into a passageway, the ground is sloped and treacherous. Every step sends a shower of grit sliding into the abyss below. About twenty meters in, the passage widens abruptly. The walls are limestone, smooth in places, razor-sharp in others. He runs a hand along the right side, feeling the ridges, the sudden dips where water cut channels for centuries.

There is no evidence of humankind. No discarded carabiners. Not frayed lengths of rope. No dropped match ends. Not a single foot print.

This is an uncharted cave.

Sweet.

He spends a few minutes exploring, crosses a wide chamber that could house several hundred people, and enters another passageway. The flashlight beam catches the edge of a glassy pool. The water is obsidian black. When he dips a finger in, the temperature is just above freezing. He takes a sip, cupping his hands. It tastes like minerals and old earth.

He clicks off the light and waits, letting his eyes adjust. After three minutes, he can see faint luminescence—moss on the rocks, or maybe some kind of bioluminescent fungus. The glow is faint, but it's enough see by.

Hours pass as he explores, sincerely hoping he doesn't cause a cave-in or disturb some ancient horror-movie beast. The cave system is bigger than he imagined. Three chambers, each connected by passageways. The first is a cathedral, easily the size of his school gym. The second is the pool room. The third, drier, studded with stalagmites. And off the passageways there are several alcoves that would make excellent individual spaces.

This place could hide an army. Or a revolution.

Kyle sleeps in the cave. Doesn't have to worry about rain. Hopes to hell the cave isn't home to modified bears or wolves or anything more terrifying. He flinches at every sound, then eventually falls asleep to the steady rhythm of dripping water.

He's up at dawn, charting the slope, counting the number of times his foot slips before the angle flattens. He memorizes all of it. Once he has the basics, he searches for exits. Matt said a true safe house needed more than one way out. He spends an hour in the third chamber, feeling along the walls for loose rocks or hidden cracks. He finds a seam behind a slab of flowstone, and with a little force, he can pry it open enough to squeeze through. The passage is tight, and he has to belly-crawl, but after twenty meters it opens onto a shelf high above the forest floor. It's camouflaged by hanging roots and ferns—impossible to see unless you know exactly where to look.

He marks the spot. Nothing that would stand out, just a notch pattern that he'll be able to recognize.

Back inside, he explores every alcove. There's one at the edge of the pool chamber—a shadowed dent in the wall, no bigger than a closet. He slips inside, pulls his knees to his chest, and feels the world shrink down to silence. It's the kind of spot you could hide in if things go bad.

Maybe it was once a bear's den. Or maybe the world made it just for him.

He retraces his path out of the cave. Once outside, he catalogs the landmarks: the triple pine trunks, the slope of the ravine, the color of the moss on the north side. He circles the area three times, making sure there's no sign of his entry. No footprints, no torn branches, nothing.

On the hike back to civilization, he moves slower, thinking about logistics. They'll need to get supplies here without drawing attention. Maybe at night, maybe using alternate routes. He wonders if he's getting paranoid. *Better paranoid than dead.*

He doesn't reach the city until dawn two days later, legs buzzing with lactic acid, eyes gritty from lack of sleep. The streetlights are still on, the world just starting to stir. Hesitating, he pauses at the edge of the Great Woods, looking back at the darkness between the trees.

He is carrying a secret the size of a mountain.

CHAPTER 6

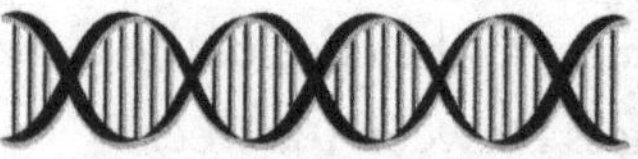

Francesca drives like she's piloting a tank through an active warzone. Kyle spends the whole ride fighting the urge to brace his arms against the dash, but he doesn't want to give her the satisfaction. Matt is in the back, blue eyes darting between the woods and his phone, running some kind of security algorithm. Claus sits perfectly still, hands folded, taking it all in with the patience of an oak.

They're an odd team, but Kyle trusts them more than anyone.

The road stops being a road after the first hour. The last three miles are a tangle of ruts and fallen limbs. Francesca guides the 4x4 up the side of a dry creek bed and parks in a bush.

"We walk from here," she says. "Quiet. No comms unless you need to."

Matt's already out, checking his pack, unfurling a paper map. "You sure the perimeter's clean?" he asks Kyle.

"Positive," Kyle says. "I checked it twice this morning. No drones, no movement."

Claus shoulders a canvas pack and nods to Kyle. "Lead on."

The hike is harder than Kyle remembers, mostly because he's used to moving at several times this speed. Every time he gets too far ahead, Francesca hisses at him to slow down. Claus struggles with the elevation, but he never complains. Matt keeps glancing at the GPS, then at the trees, like he expects the bogeyman to jump out at him.

They follow the faint line of the stream, cross the ridge, and descend the valley slope. The woods are quieter today, maybe because of the heat, maybe because the animals can sense something about their intent.

When they reach the clump of pine trees, Kyle stops, catches his breath, and looks at the others. They give him small nods, so he pushes aside the tangle of vines and gestures to the slit in the earth. "Here."

Matt's eyebrows lift. "Good find."

Kyle watches their faces, searching for signs of approval, disappointment, anything. Francesca's expression remains neutral. Claus strokes his mustache, eyes narrowed in assessment. Matt's gaze is already calculating angles, distances, vulnerabilities.

Francesca checks an ordinance survey map. "It's not listed."

Kyle grins. "Which means no one knows it's here."

Their smiles widen. Then they edge through the opening, switching on flashlights, beams cutting through the darkness. The temperature drops immediately, cool limestone surrounding them as the passage narrows, then opens into the main chamber.

"Watch your step here," he warns as they descend deeper. "It gets slippery."

"We could add some planks," Matt murmurs, mostly to himself. "Megan's wheelchair could fit."

They arrive in the main chamber.

Francesca's flashlight beam sweeps across the open space. "We could house at least five hundred people here," she notes, her voice echoing against the stone. "With proper organization."

"The lake provides fresh water," Kyle says, leading them in that direction. He flicks his beam across the surface. "I've tested it. It's clean."

Francesca nods. "We'd need filtration systems. Purification tablets at minimum."

"Power will be the biggest challenge," Matt adds, eyes scanning the ceiling. "Solar is out of the question unless we run cables from somewhere discrete above ground."

"Generators," Francesca suggests. "We could muffle the sound with proper insulation."

"What about ventilation?" Claus asks, his accent thicker in the enclosed space. "With many people, air becomes a problem."

Matt points to where the ceiling rises toward natural chimneys. "There's airflow. We'd need to enhance it, but it's workable. And we could use those chimneys to cook."

"The location is ideal," Francesca says, gesturing toward the forest they've just traveled through. "Far enough from

Central City to be considered irrelevant, but close enough to be accessible."

"No drone routes overhead," Matt adds. "I checked the patrol maps before we left."

Claus places a hand on Kyle's shoulder. "You have found something valuable, Kyle-kun."

Kyle exhales, unaware he'd been holding his breath. "So, we can use it?"

Matt turns to him, his bright blue eyes reflecting the flashlight beam. "This place is perfect, Kyle. Hidden, defensible, and large enough for our needs."

Francesca is making notes on a small, offline tablet. "We'll need to establish supply lines. Carefully. No patterns that could be tracked."

"I can help with that," Kyle offers quickly. "I can make multiple trips and take different routes each time."

"We should map the entire system," Francesca says, gesturing to the passages branching off the main chamber. "There could be other entrances we don't know about. Potential vulnerabilities."

"Or escape routes," Claus adds.

Kyle watches as they move around the space, already claiming it with their plans and ideas. For the first time since joining the resistance, he feels like he's contributed something truly valuable. Something that can't be traced back to his parents or his status. Something that's entirely his. He made this possible.

"When do we start?" he asks.

"Tomorrow," Francesca decides. "We'll bring a small team first. Essential supplies only."

Kyle weaves through the trees, a duffel bag slung over each shoulder. The Great Woods swallow sound, leaving only the soft crunch of leaves beneath his feet and the distant call of birds. His muscles buzz with nanite-fueled energy, begging to be unleashed at full speed, but he keeps his pace measured.

Matt's warnings echo in his head: *Don't make a path. Don't leave a trace. Don't be predictable.*

He shifts direction again, cutting west where he previously went east. The trees grow denser here, pine needles cushioning his steps. He pauses at the ridgeline, spends a few minutes making sure the valley is empty, then speeds toward the copse of trees that hide the cave's entrance.

"More blankets," he announces one he's made it inside, dropping the duffels at Francesca's feet. "And the medical supplies Matt requested."

"Put the meds with the others. Eastern alcove. Blankets go in the north corner." Francesca doesn't look up from her inventory list. "Thanks, Kyle."

Smiling, Kyle hefts the bags again and navigates deeper into the cave. Three weeks ago, this place was empty stone and echoes. Now it's like a second home. Maybe a first, considering he doesn't like being at his real home too much.

Battery-powered lanterns hang from hooks drilled into the rock, the warm lights eating away at the darkness. Plastic tarps subdivide the alcoves and smaller chambers into private spaces. Crates of supplies line the walls.

He finds Matt crouched near one of the smaller chambers, wiring something into the stone.

"How's the perimeter coming?" Kyle asks, pausing beside him.

Matt squints at a connection. "Slower than I'd like. These need to be invisible but effective." He glances up. "One more trip to the warehouse tonight. I need the rest of the motion sensors and the signal jammers."

"I can do it."

Matt shakes his head. "Too risky for you to go twice so often. I'll handle it."

Kyle wants to argue but swallows the urge. Matt's right—his face is too recognizable, his absence too noticeable if he's gone too long. He's told his parents that Claus has been taking him on trips to help prepare for an upcoming competition. He's had to put off the reporter shadow they suggested.

He continues toward the eastern alcove, where a makeshift medical station is taking shape. Clear plastic bins labeled with Francesca's handwriting: BANDAGES, ANTIBIOTICS, PAINKILLERS, SURGICAL.

He unpacks the supplies, organizing items according to the system already in place. His speed makes him efficient, but he's learning to channel it into precision rather than just raw velocity. Claus' training bleeds into everything now.

"Kyle-kun," Claus calls from across the chamber. "When you finish, I need help with the supports."

Kyle completes his task and joins his sensei at the far end of the smaller chamber, where Claus is reinforcing a section of low ceiling with wooden beams.

"Hold this end," Claus instructs, positioning Kyle beneath a beam. "Steady."

Kyle plants his feet in the stance Claus has drilled into

him for years. The weight of the beam settles across his palms. While Claus secures the other end, Kyle studies the space his sensei has already transformed. A flat area cleared of rocks, its floor covered with interlocking foam mats salvaged from a closed community center. Wooden training dummies stand at one end, their arms positioned at different angles for blocking practice.

"You've built a dojo," Kyle says, surprised.

Claus nods once. "Resistance is not only about running or hiding. It is about standing your ground when necessary." He tightens a brace with a few efficient turns of a wrench. "Unadjusteds must learn to defend themselves. Altereds must learn control."

When the beam is secure, they move to the next section. Kyle helps Claus place crash pads against particularly jagged walls, making the training area safer.

"The water system needs checking," Claus says when they finish. "Matt is concerned about contamination."

Kyle nods and makes his way toward the underground lake. Matt has rigged a simple filtration system—plastic pipes drawing water through layers of charcoal, sand, and fabric into large storage containers. Kyle tests the connections, tightening where needed, then fills a sample jar for testing.

The cave transforms with each passing day. What began as empty space now contains the seeds of something... *more*. Sleeping areas with foam mattresses and thermal blankets. A communications hub where Matt monitors police bands and government channels. Food storage stacked with non-perishables. A strategy table where Francesca spreads maps and plans supply runs. It's not long until summer break, and Kyle can't wait to attend the advanced altered karate camp his parents signed a fake piece of paper for. He'll be here, living his new life.

Kyle is standing in the main chamber, surveying their progress, when Matt approaches. He stands beside Kyle, offers him a protein bar.

"I can't believe this place," Kyle says, unwrapping the bar. "When I joined, I thought we'd just be passing pamphlets or something."

Matt's laugh is brief. "This isn't a high school protest, Kyle. This is survival." He gestures at the cave around them. "President Bear is planning something big. We need to be ready."

"You really think he's going to force people to take nanites?"

"I know he is. And when he does, the unadjusteds need somewhere safe to go."

"It's not big enough for all the unadjusteds."

"This isn't the only safe house."

Kyle gapes at him.

"The operation is far bigger than our little warehouse. It spans the country."

"Jeez..."

Matt chuckles, then says, "You better get home. You said your parents were expecting you for dinner?"

Kyle rolls his eyes. "Some bullshit new program or nanite they want to talk about."

Matt puts a hand on his shoulder. "It's not time wasted. You're our ears and eyes. Don't forget that."

Kyle gets to his feet, brushes himself off, and says

goodbye to his team. Then he speeds through the forest all the way back to central city. He has time to grab a shower before his parents get home and to throw his clothes in the wash to hide the evidence of the woods.

He is freshly dressed when his parents arrive and whisk him away to a restaurant downtown. More solar-grilled skyfish, probably.

He's never been to this restaurant before and it's a hot mess of glass and chrome and shifting colors. It gives him a headache.

"Darling, you've barely touched your protein supplement," his mother says, gesturing to the green swirl in his glass. "Your body needs the extra nutrients to maintain that wonderful speed of yours."

Kyle takes a sip to appease her. It tastes like chemicals. He wouldn't put it past her to slip him more nanites without his consent.

"Sorry, Mom. Just thinking about that calculus test tomorrow." The lie slips out easily. He's been doing it for weeks now.

His father scrolls through his tablet, not looking up. "I've confirmed your appearance at the Youth Enhancement Summit next month. President Bear will be speaking, and they want you for the demonstration portion." The pride in his voice causes the protein drink to bubble back up Kyle's throat. "It's prime visibility. National broadcast."

"Sounds great," Kyle says, mustering some enthusiasm. Six months ago, the prospect of standing beside President Bear would have filled him with genuine excitement. Now, the thought makes him sick.

His mother beams at him across the table. "Your follower count jumped another twenty thousand after your last race footage went viral. The sponsors are practically begging for exclusive contracts." She reaches for her wine glass, the liquid inside the exact shade of blood. "I'm thinking we leverage that for the summer campaign. Your father says the timing will be perfect with what's coming."

Kyle's fork pauses halfway to his mouth. "What's coming?"

His parents exchange a loaded glance.

His father sets down his tablet. "The President is finalizing a new initiative. Broader access to higher-class nanites for those who qualify. More comprehensive integration programs in schools and workplaces." His voice drops lower, confidential. "And eventually, mandatory baseline enhancements for all citizens."

"Mandatory?" Kyle repeats. The word sits heavy on his tongue. This is what Matt's been talking about.

"It's for the greater good, sweetheart," his mother says, smoothing her napkin. "Just think—no more inequality in basic capabilities. No more children left behind simply because their parents can't afford entry-level enhancements."

Kyle's hand tightens around his fork. He thinks of the warehouse meetings, of unadjusteds with fierce pride in their unaltered bodies. Of Silver's cuff. Of Matt's words: choice is what makes us human.

"Doesn't mandatory mean no choice?" he asks, keeping his tone light, curious rather than confrontational.

His father laughs. "Choice is overrated when it comes to societal advancement, son. Did people choose to receive vaccines a century ago? Did they choose clean water systems? Some things transcend individual preference." He cuts into his fat, lab-grown steak. "Besides, we're only talking about basic enhancements. Class 3 at most. Nothing that fundamentally changes identity—just improves function. Reduces crime rates. Increases work productivity."

Kyle's heart hammers against his ribs. Class 3 nanites include the butterfly wings some of the resistance members bear. Include things like increased processing speeds and reflexes and stamina. Modifications that absolutely change the course of lives.

"What about people who don't want to change?" he asks.

His mother sighs. "Those people are living in the past, Kyle. Afraid of progress. It's like refusing electricity because candles were good enough for your grandparents." She reaches across the table to pat his hand. "Don't worry. There will be educational programs to help them understand the benefits."

"Re-education, you mean," Kyle says before he can stop himself.

His father's eyebrows lift. "That's a loaded term. Where did you pick that up?"

Kyle backpedals quickly. "Just something we discussed in history class. About resistance to change throughout human development."

"Well, this isn't about forcing people," his father says, though his eyes remain suspicious. "It's about creating a stronger nation. President Bear understands that our global position depends on having the most advanced population. Other countries are catching up with nanite technology. We can't afford to fall behind because some people cling to outdated notions of *natural* humanity."

Kyle nods, as if this makes perfect sense. Inside, his stomach churns. The resistance was right. It's coming faster than they thought.

"When will this program start?" he asks carefully.

"The first phase rolls out next month," his father says. "Your mother and I are part of the advanced publicity team. That's why your appearances are so important—you represent the perfect success story."

"The golden boy," his mother adds, pride lighting her artificial eyes. "Proof that enhancement only brings out what was already there."

Kyle forces himself to smile. "I'm happy to help." The lie tastes as bitter as the protein smoothie.

"That's why we love you," his father says, returning to his tablet. "Always a team player."

The conversation shifts to his mother's latest social media campaign, something about "Evolution Now" that's trending in fourteen countries. Kyle nods in all the right places, asks appropriate questions, plays the role they expect. But his mind catalogs every detail about the upcoming program, mentally composing the report he'll deliver to Francesca and Matt and Claus.

Who are these people? The thought strikes him as he watches his parents discuss human enhancement as casually as interior decorating. Have they always been this blind, this callous? Or has he been the blind one, willfully ignoring the snowballing shit?

His mother laughs at something his father says. They

clink glasses in a toast to "the future," and Kyle raises his protein shake in false solidarity.

These strangers across the table—they've crafted him, marketed him, sold his speed to the highest bidder. And now they plan to do the same to everyone else, willing or not.

When dinner finally ends, Kyle excuses himself to study. In his room, he stares at the Jacob Shea digi-posters on his walls—once inspiration, now propaganda. Tomorrow, they come down. Tomorrow, he smuggles what he's learned to the cave. Tomorrow, he becomes the spy in his own home.

Tonight, he mourns the parents he thought he had.

CHAPTER 7

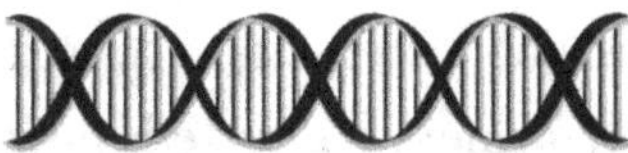

KYLE COUNTS the empty desks as he walks the main hallway. Three more gone this week. Three more unadjusteds who couldn't keep up with the increasing number of altereds in the world. Parents fired and moved away. Kids bullied or drowning in academics. Maybe some of them have even gone into hiding.

There are more wings in the halls. More bulks. More horns. More speed. More muscle. More everything. Kyle is a little horrified himself. If he weren't already making plans for a different future, maybe he would flee now too.

A girl with iridescent skin brushes past him, her laugh tinkling like programmed wind chimes. She wasn't here yesterday. Mira Stevens' seat was empty yesterday—the quiet unadjusted girl who sketched birds during lunch period. Now this shimmering creature occupies her space like she's always belonged there.

Kyle keeps his face neutral, his famous practiced smile plastered to his lips. Inside, his stomach knots. He spots another new face where Ben Holloway once sat—a boy with unnaturally bright eyes and fingers that move too quickly as he unpacks his tablet. Ben's parents couldn't afford the intelligence nanite the school recommended last month. Now he's gone. Vanished like he never existed.

The bell rings, adding to Kyle's now constant headache. He slides into his chemistry class, conscious of two more substitutions—both former unadjusteds now sporting the telltale signs of recent enhancement. One boy's neck pulses with a new digi-tattoo.

Mr. Patterson clears his throat at the front of the room. "Before we begin our lesson on molecular reconfiguration, I have an announcement. Next week, we'll be hosting a special nanite education assembly. Attendance is mandatory."

The word hits Kyle like a slap. *Mandatory.* Just like his father said at dinner.

"Representatives from NanoTech will be presenting the latest advancements in educational enhancement options." Patterson smiles with too many teeth. "A wonderful opportunity for those of you still considering your optimal enhancement path."

Translation: a final warning for the remaining unadjusteds.

Kyle's fingers curl around his stylus, squeezing until his knuckles whiten. Two rows ahead, a girl with unaltered features sinks lower in her seat. Her shoulders curve inward, making herself smaller. Invisible. It won't work for long.

"Additionally," Patterson continues, "I'm pleased to announce that Kyle Lewis will be demonstrating the benefits of speed enhancement during the presentation."

Heads turn toward him. Kyle forces his face into the expected grin, giving the class a small wave. His publicity smile. The one his mother taught him. The one that now gives him a near constant migraine.

"Looking forward to it," he lies, voice steady despite the rage bubbling beneath his ribs.

The class dissolves into lab work. Kyle goes through the motions, measuring compounds, recording results, maintaining his carefully constructed facade. But his mind races. He needs to warn Francesca. The timeline is accelerating.

After class, he makes his way to the library. Kyle navigates to the far corner, ancient physical books on theoretical physics creating a natural shield from prying eyes. Matt already waits there, sandy hair falling across his forehead as he pretends to read something on quantum mechanics. Or, knowing him, maybe he really is reading it.

Kyle slides into the chair opposite him, opening a random textbook. Their eyes meet briefly.

"Three more gone this week," Kyle says, keeping his voice low. "Replaced by perfect little altereds."

Matt doesn't look up from his book. "One of my neighbors disappeared yesterday." His finger traces a meaningless pattern on the page. "Second one on our block this month."

"They're accelerating the program," Kyle whispers. "Assembly next week. 'Educational opportunities' with NanoTech reps."

"Recruitment or enforcement?"

"Both. They want me to demonstrate." Kyle's jaw tightens. "My father mentioned mandatory enhancements starting soon. Class 3 minimum."

Matt's fingers freeze on the page. "How soon?"

"Next quarter officially. But I think it's already happening. These new students—they all have the same look. Like they came off an assembly line."

"Francesca thinks—" Matt starts, then cuts himself off.

Kyle leans forward. "What does Francesca think?"

"That they're testing compliance levels. The ones who resist disappear first."

A shadow falls across their table.

"Homework help again, Lewis?" Jax's voice carries that new resonance—the bulk nanite altering his vocal cords along with everything else. How many has he taken now? "Or something else?"

Kyle raises his head slowly, casual, unbothered. Jax barely fits between the bookshelves now, his enhanced frame stretching his Central City High uniform across shoulders twice their natural width. His eyes have that metallic sheen of multiple enhancements.

"Hey, Jax," Kyle says, leaning back in his chair. "Just catching up on some quantum theory. You know how it is."

Jax's enhanced eyes narrow, focusing not on Kyle but on Matt. "Didn't know you two were study buddies."

Kyle shifts slightly, blocking Matt from Jax's direct line of sight.

"Tutoring," Kyle says with a practiced shrug. "Mr. Patterson paired us up. Trying to bring everyone's scores up before finals."

"Right." Jax's mouth twists into something that resembles a smile. "Wouldn't want anyone falling behind the curve."

The threat hangs in the air between them. Kyle feels

Matt tense beside him, but he doesn't break eye contact with Jax.

"Exactly," Kyle says, voice light. "I'm all about the speed, not the academics."

Jax leans against the bookshelf, wood creaking under his enhanced weight. "You're still coming to the Youth Enforcers meeting tonight, right? President Bear's special envoy will be there. Said he specifically asked for you."

The invitation sounds like a test. One that Kyle has no intention of passing.

"Can't make it," he says, maintaining his easy smile. "Family dinner. My dad's orders."

"Your *dad*." Jax studies him, head tilted. "Funny. He asked *my* dad if you were still attending the meetings. Seemed concerned about your... commitment."

Ice slides down Kyle's spine. His father is checking up on him.

"Scheduling mix-up," Kyle says smoothly. "You know how it is with all the appearances they book for me."

Jax holds his gaze a moment longer, then straightens. "Sure thing, golden boy. Whatever you say." He takes a step back, his shoulders knocking a few books onto the floor. "See you at the assembly. I'll be demonstrating too. Bulk capabilities." His eyes flick to Matt. "Should be educational for everyone."

As Jax disappears around the corner, Kyle exhales slowly. Matt's fingers have gone white against his book.

"He suspects something," Matt whispers.

Kyle nods. "We need to move faster."

〼〼〼

Kyle stands in front of the mirror adjusting the tie his mother laid out for him—crimson silk against a shirt so white it hurts his eyes. The Youth Leadership Conference starts in thirty minutes. His speech is saved on his phone, words crafted by his father's PR team.

He won't be delivering it. Not tonight.

He waits until his parents leave. First, his father in the sleek government car, then his mother following in her own vehicle to capture arrival footage for her EvolveMe stream. Then he changes quickly into dark clothing, hiding his face beneath a nondescript hood. No one can know Central City's golden boy is out mapping enemy territory tonight.

The city blurs around him as he activates his speed. He moves through alleyways and service corridors, places without cameras or with blind spots he's already memorized.

At the edge of the industrial district, he slows. The NanoTech distribution center rises before him—a gleaming fortress of steel and glass, soft blue light pulsing from within. This is where it happens. Where the pills that rebuild humanity are sorted, classified, and shipped to waiting recipients.

Kyle perches on a rooftop across the street, concealing himself in the shadows. He counts the guards—twelve visible, likely more inside. Notes the patrol patterns—overlapping sweeps, each lasting exactly eight minutes and twenty seconds. Identifies the camera blind spots—minimal, but present if you know where to look. He spots the reflective blink of motion sensors, the reinforced access panels, the weight-sensitive plates embedded in the tarmac.

Three trucks enter the compound while he watches. Each undergoes the same inspection protocol: scanning, cataloging, verification of digital and physical seals. Kyle commits every detail to memory. The resistance doesn't have cameras or tablets for this kind of reconnaissance—too risky, too traceable. Information travels in whispers only.

A drone passes overhead. Kyle freezes, pressing himself flatter against the rooftop. His heart hammers. If he's caught here, there's no explanation that saves him. No excuse his father can spin. No future except disappearance.

The drone moves on. Kyle exhales. Checks his watch. It's nearly time for the rendezvous.

He drops from the rooftop to the alley below. Three blocks east, two north. Moving fast.

The convenience store sits on the corner, its lights flickering unevenly across cracked pavement. Kyle circles around to the back, where the security camera has been carefully angled away from one specific corner.

She's already waiting. The woman has no name, at least not one Kyle knows. Her cheeks are hollow, eyes too large in her thin face. An unadjusted working in food service, one of thousands pushed to the economic margins as enhanced workers take the better positions.

"You're late," she says, throwing a cigarette on the pavement.

"Drone patrol," Kyle replies, then leans closer to her, even though she stinks of French Fries. And not the tasty kind. "The shipment comes Thursday," he whispers. "Three trucks, western entrance. Twenty-two hundred hours. Class Eight and above. Minimal marking."

Her eyes widen—the only indication of her surprise. Class Eight nanites are rare, restricted, powerful. She nods once, then melts into the darkness between buildings.

Kyle takes a different route home, doubling back twice to ensure he isn't followed. The sky has darkened to pitch by the time he slips through his bedroom window, the conference long over. He's peeling off his hoodie when the light clicks on.

His father sits in the chair by Kyle's desk, eyes cold as winter glass. He's still wearing his conference suit, the NanoTech pin gleaming on his lapel like an accusation.

"You embarrassed me tonight," his father says, voice level in a way that signals danger more clearly than shouting ever could. "Do you understand what you've done?"

Kyle stands straighter, letting the hoodie fall to the floor. No point hiding it now. "I wasn't feeling well."

"Don't." His father cuts him off with a sharp gesture. "Don't insult us both with lies. You weren't sick. You weren't injured. You simply decided that your commitment to your *family*, to this *administration*, to your *future*, wasn't worth honoring tonight."

"It was just one appearance," Kyle says.

His father stands, straightening his already perfect cuffs. "The President's Chief of Staff was there. The head of NanoTech's Youth Division was there. Everyone who matters in shaping the next phase was there." He takes a step closer. "Everyone except the one young man I promised would demonstrate what enhanced loyalty looks like."

The irony of the phrase doesn't escape Kyle. *Enhanced*

loyalty. As if devotion comes in a pill now too. Maybe it does. Kyle doesn't look at the commercials anymore.

"I'm sorry," Kyle says. And he is. He's sorry it's come to this. He's sorry they don't see eye to eye. He's sorry his parents are the people they are.

His father studies him, eyes narrowed. "This isn't a phase, Kyle. It's your duty. Your responsibility." He adjusts his NanoTech pin. "People are counting on you. More than you know."

The weight of the double meaning presses down on Kyle's shoulders. His father thinks he means the administration, the program, the perfect future they're building on the backs of the unadjusted. But Kyle feels the truth of it differently—the people in the warehouse, in the cave, the ones disappearing from classrooms and neighborhoods. They're counting on him too.

"I understand my responsibilities," Kyle says, meeting his father's gaze.

Something flickers across his father's face—doubt, perhaps, or the first inkling that his perfect son might be developing thoughts of his own.

"I hope you do." His father moves toward the door, then pauses. "Your mother has arranged a reshoot for tomorrow's EvolveMe stream. You will be present, you will be enthusiastic, and you will make up for tonight's lapse." It's not a request.

Kyle says nothing, just holds his father's gaze with silent defiance.

After his father leaves, Kyle sits on the edge of his bed, hands trembling from the confrontation. The double life is getting harder to maintain. The lies are piling up, building walls between who he pretends to be and who he's becoming.

But he remembers the hollow-cheeked woman, remembers the empty desks at school, remembers Silver's cuff. He remembers Diana's death that no one talks about anymore. The system is accelerating, tightening its grip.

Despite his exhaustion, Kyle doesn't sleep. He has no intention of attending the EvolveMe shoot, but he hasn't figured out how to get out of it. Yet.

As the day progresses, and more people fill the house with cameras and microphones and makeup and other stuff he can't identify, the more he experiences the urge to run.

"The Lewis family, perfect in every way," his mother chirps, turquoise eyes gleaming as she fusses with Kyle's collar. Her fingers are cool against his neck. "This livestream could hit eight million views. The President's office specifically requested we emphasize the educational benefits of your speed enhancement."

Kyle nods, throat tight. Yesterday's missed appearance hangs between them, unmentioned but not forgotten. His father stands nearby, adjusting the knot of his tie in a decorative mirror. The script sits on the coffee table—three pages of carefully crafted propaganda about "choice" and "opportunity" and "the future." All lies.

"I need some air," Kyle says suddenly. "Just five minutes."

His mother frowns, glancing at her watch. "The livestream begins in twenty minutes. We still need to do your final touch-up."

"Five minutes," Kyle repeats, already backing toward the

door. "Promise." He's gone before anyone can tell him otherwise.

Outside, the evening air is a relief to his lungs. Kyle jogs down the manicured path of their front garden, mind racing. He can't do this. Can't sit on that perfect white couch and sell more lies to more people who don't know what's happening to the unadjusteds. Can't be the face of a system that's making classmates disappear.

He reaches the decorative stone wall that marks the property boundary and stops. What he's considering is desperate. Stupid, even. But necessary.

Kyle looks around, confirming no security cameras are angled in his direction. Then he takes a deep breath, steels himself, and drives his own fist into his face—once, twice. Pain explodes across his cheekbone. He's careful to pull the punch just enough to avoid serious damage but not enough to prevent visible bruising.

He waits thirty seconds, letting the bruise darken, feeling his eye swell. Then he messes up his hair, tears his shirt at the collar, and limps back to the house.

His mother screams when he stumbles through the door. "Kyle! What happened?"

"Some guys jumped me," he gasps, hand pressed to his face. "Three of them. Came out of nowhere."

His father rushes forward, tilting Kyle's face toward the light. "Where? Who were they?"

"Didn't see faces," Kyle mumbles. "Happened too fast."

His mother's hands flutter around him, not quite touching the bruise. "But your speed—you should have been able to—"

"They surprised me," Kyle cuts in. "I wasn't... I wasn't paying attention."

His father's eyes narrow, studying the injury. "And you didn't fight back? With your enhancements?"

Kyle swallows. "It happened so fast. They ran off when someone shouted from a house nearby."

The lie sits between them, fragile as spun glass. His father's jaw tightens—he doesn't believe it. How could he? Kyle's speed makes him nearly impossible to ambush, and his reflexes should have protected him from any ordinary attack.

His mother, however, is focused on a different crisis. "The livestream," she says, voice rising. "We can't possibly broadcast with you looking like this. What will people think? That Central City isn't safe? That enhancements don't protect our children?"

"We'll have to reschedule," his father says, still watching Kyle with calculated suspicion.

"Reschedule? The President's media team coordinated this timing specifically to precede next week's announcement!" His mother's voice climbs higher. "This is a disaster. A complete disaster."

She stalks to her phone, already dialing her publicist. "Yes, hello, we have an emergency situation. Kyle's been attacked. No, he's fine, but his face is—yes, exactly. We need damage control immediately. Spin it as a random incident, nothing to do with—"

Kyle walks away as she continues, retreating to his room. He catches his father's stare following him up the stairs. The suspicion in that gaze sends a chill down Kyle's spine. How long before his father stops giving him the benefit of the doubt? How long before the questions become accusations?

In his room, Kyle examines his handiwork in the mirror. The bruise blooms purple beneath his left eye, swelling impressively. Worth it. One more night of freedom from being the regime's poster boy.

After his parents go to bed, Kyle slips out the window again. He carries messages too dangerous to trust to any digital system—locations of safe houses, names of sympathetic doctors, warnings about increased patrols in certain sectors. The resistance network spreads beneath the glossy surface of Central City like roots beneath pavement, connecting those who still believe in choice.

Kyle lands silently on a fire escape, then descends to the alley below. His contact here works in city planning—an unadjusted woman whose access to infrastructure maps has given them a huge advantage. He taps a precise pattern against her window—three quick, two slow.

The window slides open just enough for a folded paper to pass through. No words exchanged. Safer that way.

Two more meets, then he can return home. Kyle scales the wall to the rooftop, calculating the fastest route to the medical district. From here, he can see President Bear's tower rising in the distance, red light pulsing at its peak like a malevolent heartbeat.

He's midway across the third rooftop when he hears it. A low, rumbling growl that doesn't belong to any animal he knows. Kyle freezes, instinctively dropping to a crouch. The sound comes again, closer this time, from the street below.

He edges forward, peering over the crumbling lip of the

roof—and what he sees twists his stomach into knots. Three massive creatures prowl the street below. Dogs—only in the loosest sense of the word—their bodies too large, massive shoulders hunched, hides rippling like molten tar over muscle. Their eyes glow a sickly yellow in the darkness, heads swinging from side to side as they scent the air, jaws lined with teeth too long, too sharp, steam curling from between them as if they breathed fire in their sleep. Kyle's breath stutters. He has no name for it, no reference in nature or nightmare. The word spills unbidden into his mind: *hellhound.*

Each beast must weigh as much as a small car, jaws designed to crush bone, claws scraping against pavement as they move. Purpose-built predators created to... hunt... and *kill?*

Their handlers, soldiers in black tactical gear, scan the surroundings.

One hellhound stops directly beneath Kyle's position, nose lifting to the air. It growls, a sound that vibrates through Kyle's chest. The handler tightens its leash, checking a device on his wrist.

"Got something?" another soldier asks.

"Residual trace. Enhanced subject moved through here recently."

Kyle's heart hammers against his ribs. They can smell his enhancement. He'd never considered that possibility.

The hellhound strains against its leash, yellowed teeth bared as it stares upward—not quite at Kyle's position, but close. *Too* close.

"Worth pursuing?" the handler asks.

The squad leader consults his tablet. "Negative. We're not here for the enhanced."

The handler yanks the hellhound's leash, forcing it to move on. The creature resists for a moment, still sensing something, before reluctantly following. Kyle remains frozen in place, barely breathing until the patrol turns the corner and disappears from sight.

Only then does he allow himself to exhale. His hands tremble as he processes what just happened. They're hunting unadjusteds now? Why? Most of them are just trying to go about their lives.

The questions multiply in his mind as he continues his mission, moving with even greater caution now. The risks are evolving faster than he can comprehend. The dangers are multiplying.

Something is changing in Central City. Something even the golden boy of the nanite revolution isn't supposed to know about.

Kyle touches his bruised eye. He can't take much more of this.

CHAPTER 8

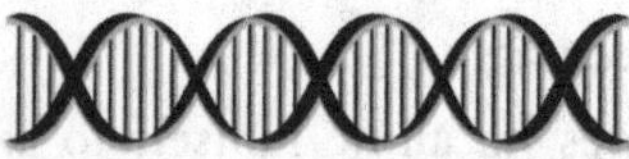

KYLE CROUCHES outside his father's office, one ear pressed to the polished wood. His parents' bedroom door hasn't opened in two hours. He checks his watch: 2:17 a.m.

Time to move.

His fingers hover over the doorknob. This is crossing a line he can't uncross. This isn't running from a publicity shoot or missing an appearance.

This is treason.

He thinks of Silver's cuff. Of empty desks in classrooms. Of hellhounds prowling streets.

Kyle turns the knob, wincing at the nearly inaudible click. The door swings open on perfectly oiled hinges. His father's office is a shrine to power—awards mounted on mahogany walls, photos with President Bear displayed prominently, the NanoTech logo etched into glass paperweights that catch moonlight from the window. The room smells of leather and whiskey.

The laptop sits on the massive desk. Kyle slides into his father's chair, the leather cool against his palms. He boots up the system. Sweat slides down his temple.

The password prompt glows. Kyle's fingers freeze above the keyboard. He's only seen his father enter it once, glimpsed over his shoulder during a rare moment of carelessness. Eight characters. His mother's initials, Kyle's birthday, and the year his father joined Bear's administration. A family code to protect state secrets.

Kyle types it in, his fingers tripping. The screen unlocks.

He navigates through folders with clinical names —"Distribution Protocols," "Enhancement Initiatives," "Class Clearances." Kyle's pulse quickens. There's so much here. All the evidence the resistance needs.

He skims through the files. Matt was clear: shipment schedules only. Times, routes, security details.

He finds it in a subfolder labeled "Q2 Logistics." A complete manifest of every nanite shipment for the next month—warehouses, transport routes, security protocols. The motherlode.

Kyle plugs in the encrypted drive Matt gave him. Sweat beads at his hairline, more drops sliding down his temple. The files copy painfully slowly. Every second is an eternity. He keeps his eyes on the doorway, alert for the shadowy movement of a parent in slippers.

The screen displays 47%... 53%... 68%...

His stomach twists. These aren't just documents. This is his father's work. His legacy. Everything he's built with President Bear. And Kyle is sabotaging it from the inside, from the chair where his father sits each morning to plan the future.

The download reaches 89% when a floorboard creaks somewhere in the house.

Kyle freezes, muscles locking into place. Another creak. Footsteps. Someone's awake.

The progress bar crawls to 94%.

The footsteps move toward the stairs. Kyle's hands hover over the keyboard, ready to abort. His heartbeat is so loud he's certain whoever is awake can hear it too.

97%.

The footsteps pause at the top of the stairs, then continue down the hallway—away from the office. The bathroom door opens and closes.

100%. Complete.

Kyle exhales. He ejects the drive, careful not to leave fingerprints, and slides it into his pocket. Now comes the harder part. He meticulously retraces his digital footsteps, erasing search history, closing folders in the exact order he opened them, resetting the system logs to show no activity. Just like how Matt showed him. He hopes like hell he's done it right.

His father's password manager blinks with an alert— someone accessed restricted files. Kyle's throat tightens. He navigates to the security settings and resets the notification history, erasing all evidence of his intrusion.

The footsteps return down the hallway. The bathroom door opens and closes again. Kyle powers down the computer, exactly as his father left it. He rises from the chair, adjusts it to its previous position, and slips toward the door.

He activates his enhanced speed, the world slowing to a crawl as he eases the door shut behind him. In less than a heartbeat, he's back in his own room, door closed, breathing hard.

He waits five minutes, listening for any disturbance in the house's rhythm. Nothing. Only the normal sounds of night.

Kyle retrieves the encrypted tablet hidden beneath a loose floorboard under his bed. It powers on with a dim glow, screen designed to minimize light emission. He connects the drive, enters the encryption key Matt taught him, and begins the upload.

The resistance's secure channel opens, invisible and untraceable. The files transfer in compressed packets, bouncing through proxies across the city before reaching Matt.

A single message appears when the transfer completes: "Received. Delete everything. Sleep well."

Sleep? Whatever.

Kyle wipes the drive, then the tablet. He returns both to their hiding places. The adrenaline is fading, leaving behind a hollow ache in his chest.

He stands at his window, staring out at the peaceful neighborhood where Central City's elite rest easy. His jaw is tight enough to crack teeth. His breathing shallow. His stomach a knot of acid.

But he's done it. Given the resistance everything they need to intercept and destroy millions of nanites before they reach distribution centers. He's sabotaged his father's work, his family's position, perhaps even President Bear's timeline for mandatory enhancements.

Kyle touches his bruised eye, the pain grounding him. "No going back now," he whispers to his reflection in the glass.

)(X)(X)(X)(

Three days after the data breach, Kyle stands in front of the pharmacy's nanite section, staring at empty shelves. Ha! They did it. They interrupted the nanite shipments and all he had to do was log on to a computer in his house.

Kyle tries not to think about what would have happened if his dad had caught him.

A handwritten sign taped to one reads "Temporarily Out of Stock - All Classes." Two security guards hover nearby, eyes tracking customers who lingers too long. One of them glances at Kyle, then does a double-take—recognition flickering across his face. Kyle turns away before the man can place him.

A woman at the counter pounds her palm against it. "What do you mean you don't know when they'll be back? My daughter's appointment is tomorrow!" Her voice cracks on the last word. The pharmacist only shrugs.

Kyle moves on, runs to school in less than a minute and arrives before the second bell rings. The hallways buzz with speculation. He catches fragments as he passes groups of students.

"—canceled my brother's intelligence upgrade—"

"—said the entire month's supply just disappeared—"

"—my dad says it's terrorists—"

In the teacher's lounge, visible through the half-open door, Mr. Patterson leans close to the chemistry teacher: "Administration's in full panic mode. Bear's office calling emergency meetings. This wasn't just some random theft."

Kyle keeps his face neutral, the way he's practiced for a thousand publicity photos. But inside, something unfamiliar expands in his chest. Not quite pride. Not quite fear. Something in between.

During lunch, all eyes turn to the news screens mounted in the cafeteria. The feed shows a crowd gathered outside a NanoTech clinic, faces twisted with confusion and anger. The anchor's voice cuts through the cafeteria chatter: "—government officials continue to downplay what appears to be a coordinated attack on nanite distribution centers across Central City. While details remain classified, sources confirm that scheduled enhancements have been postponed indefinitely until supply chains can be secured—"

Jax drops his tray beside Kyle's. "Crazy, right? Some of the girls were literally crying this morning when they found out their wing nanites weren't coming."

Kyle shrugs, pushing food around his plate. "Guess they'll have to wait."

"My dad says it's those unadjusted freaks." Jax leans closer, lowering his voice. "Says they're getting organized. Starting to fight back."

Kyle's stomach tightens. "Maybe they just want a choice."

Jax's eyes narrow. "You're still hanging around that Lawson kid, aren't you? The one whose girlfriend wears the cuff?"

"Silver's not his girlfriend," Kyle says automatically, then immediately regrets engaging.

"Whatever." Jax stands, towering over Kyle. "Just be careful who you associate with. People are watching."

After school, Kyle walks through Central City's downtown. The government district thrums with unusual activity. Black vehicles with tinted windows line the curbs outside NanoTech headquarters. Security presence has doubled overnight—uniformed officers at every corner, drones hovering at key intersections.

Outside one government building, Kyle pauses to tie his shoe, ears tuned to two officials speaking just inside the glass doors.

"—entire inventory for Sector Seven, gone—"

"—someone had the exact schedule—"

"—Bear wants answers by tomorrow, or heads will roll—"

Kyle continues walking, hands in his pockets to hide their trembling. This is bigger than he imagined. Not just a disruption, but a genuine blow to the system. For the first time in years, the administration seems vulnerable.

Digital billboards throughout the city display a new message on rotation with regular advertisements: "ENHANCEMENT SERVICES TEMPORARILY DELAYED. THANK YOU FOR YOUR PATIENCE." The careful wording is most likely his father's handiwork.

When Kyle returns home, the atmosphere is charged. Tense, like the air before a storm. His father's office door stands open—unusual enough to make Kyle pause. Inside, his father paces, phone pressed to his ear, free hand gesturing sharply as if the person on the other end could see his frustration.

"—don't care what it takes. Find the leak." His father's voice is steel wrapped in silk. "Someone knew exactly where and when. This wasn't random."

Kyle retreats to his room. He sits on his bed and picks up his karate belt from the nightstand. He traces the stitching, finding the worn spots from years of training.

Hours later, darkness pools in the corners of his room. Kyle should be sleeping, but instead he lies awake, listening to the angry murmur of voices from downstairs. His parents rarely argue—they're too media-trained, too conscious of appearances—but tonight, their tight voices sound like shattering glass.

"How could this happen?" His mother's voice oozes through the floorboards, sharp with panic. "Do you understand what this does to our position? To our influence?"

His father's response is clipped. "Someone leaked the schedule. Someone with access."

"One of yours?"

"Or one of Bear's. We're checking everyone."

Kyle's stomach knots. He presses a hand against his abdomen, feeling the muscles contract beneath his palm. Will they suspect him?

"What about the assembly next week?" His mother again. "If we can't distribute the promised nanites—"

"Postponed. Everything's postponed."

Silence falls. Then his mother, softer now: "This is bad, isn't it?"

"Yes." A single syllable.

Kyle rolls onto his side, curling around the guilt that should consume him but somehow doesn't. He closes his eyes and sees Diana again—her body convulsing on the hallway floor, foam spilling from her lips, eyes rolling back as the nanite tore through her system. He remembers how quickly the news disappeared, how the school memorial lasted one day before everyone moved on, how his parents dismissed it as "an isolated incident."

His fingers find the seams of his karate belt again. He thinks of Silver's cuff, of Matt's determined face, of Francesca's fierce eyes, of Claus' quiet wisdom.

"I'm sorry, Dad," he whispers to the darkness. "*Not* sorry."

Kyle slips out his bedroom window at midnight, the drop to the ground barely registering as he dashes into the shadows. He avoids the glow of streetlamps and the watchful eyes of security cameras. His route is deliberate—alleyways, service corridors, abandoned lots—places the privileged of Central City never see. He knows them all now, has mapped them in his mind during weeks of resistance work.

He cuts through the industrial district, where factories huddle like sleeping giants. The resistance warehouse appears ahead, a hulking shadow.

Kyle approaches the east entrance, tapping out the recognition pattern against the metal door. A moment passes, then the door opens just enough to let him slip inside.

The interior is dimly lit by portable lamps positioned at strategic intervals. Matt, Francesca, and Claus wait in the center of the space, faces grave in the weak light. No one smiles. This isn't a night for pleasantries.

"Everything okay?" Francesca asks.

Kyle nods. There's not much to say.

Matt turns to the map spread across a makeshift table. His finger traces a route through Central City's industrial zone. "Warehouse 7. Minimal security—two guards at the entrance, one patrolling the perimeter. No internal surveillance beyond the main storage area."

"The information you provided was perfect," Francesca tells Kyle, her eyes holding his for a beat longer than necessary. "We confirmed this is the location that houses the reserve supply."

Matt continues. "Your information gives us time for the next phase."

Francesca moves to a duffel bag in the corner, unzipping it to reveal equipment. "We go in silent. We plant the devices. We leave no trace of who was there." She distributes items: black gloves, masks, small fuel canisters, and what Kyle recognizes as incendiary devices—handcrafted, nothing that could be traced to a manufacturer. Which is Matt. He knows how to make bombs.

Kyle takes his share, fingers closing around the cold metal of a device. This isn't information theft anymore. This is direct action. Destruction. His throat dries out.

"Your speed makes you our point person," Matt says, handing Kyle a small communication device. "You scout ahead, signal when it's clear."

"If you feel uncertain, if you wish to back out, now is the time," Claus says, his blue eyes finding Kyle's. "After tonight, there is no returning to before."

Kyle thinks of his father pacing in his office, of empty shelves in pharmacies, of Diana's body convulsing on the floor. Of Silver's cuff. Of the hellhounds prowling the streets.

"I'm in," he says. "All the way."

They move through the night like ghosts, four shadows flowing between buildings and under bridges. The city sleeps around them, unaware of the small rebellion passing through its arteries.

Warehouse 7 rises before them, a massive concrete structure with steel reinforcements. Unlike the resistance's base, this building is pristine—no graffiti, no broken windows, nothing to suggest neglect. A chain-link fence topped with razor wire surrounds the perimeter. Security lights illuminate the entrance where two guards stand at attention, rifles slung across their chests.

"Government property," Francesca whispers, crouching beside Kyle behind a loading dock across the street.

"Until tonight," Matt adds.

Kyle spots the lone patrolling guard, moving along the fence line at a steady pace. He calculates the timing, then nods to the others. "Thirty seconds between passes on the south side. That's our window."

They split into pairs—Kyle with Claus, Matt with Francesca. The guard rounds the corner, disappearing from view. Kyle and Claus approach the fence. He lifts his sensei over the razor wire, then leaps it himself with a speedy run up. They land silently on the other side just as Matt and Francesca join them.

The patrol guard turns the corner, flashlight beam sweeping the ground. All four press against the warehouse wall, breath held. The beam passes inches from their feet, then continues on. They exhale as one.

Kyle points to the side entrance—a service door likely used by maintenance staff. Matt moves forward, tools already in hand. The lock yields to his expertise in seconds. They slip inside, into darkness that smells of metal and chemicals.

The warehouse interior stretches out before them—row after row of storage units containing millions of nanites. The future of Central City's population, neatly packaged in temperature-controlled containers. The soft hum of cooling systems fills the air.

A guard appears at the end of the aisle, back turned to them. Francesca moves first, silent as a shadow. The taser in her hand connects with the guard's neck. He drops without a sound, muscles seizing then going slack. With Matt's help, she drags him behind a storage unit, zip-ties his wrists and ankles.

The second guard appears near the main entrance, radio in hand. Kyle catches Claus' eye, a silent communication passing between them. They move in tandem, years of dojo training evident in their synchronized approach. The guard turns, spots them, reaches for his weapon—too late.

Claus strikes first, a precise chop to the forearm that sends the gun clattering to the floor. Kyle follows with a sweep that takes the man's legs out from under him. Before he can shout, Claus delivers a strike to the base of his skull. Unconscious, not dead.

"Clear," Kyle calls softly.

Matt works quickly at the security panel, bypassing the

alarm system. "We have twenty minutes before the system requires a manual reset. After that, it'll trigger automatically."

They move through the warehouse, placing incendiary devices at strategic points—storage units containing the highest-class nanites, structural supports, electrical systems. Kyle's speed allows him to cover twice the ground.

The timer is set for eight minutes—enough time to clear the area, not enough time for anyone to discover their handiwork.

"Ready," Francesca announces, the last device in place.

They exit the way they came, careful to leave the unconscious guards in positions where the flames won't reach them. Outside the fence, they retreat to a vantage point behind an abandoned loading dock.

"Three minutes," Matt says, checking his watch.

No one speaks. Kyle's heart pounds against his ribs, each beat a question: Is this right? Is this necessary?

The first explosion tears through the silence like a thunderclap. Orange light blooms from within the warehouse, windows shattering outward in a cascade of glass. The second blast follows immediately, then the third—a chain reaction of destruction rippling through the structure. Flames engulf the building with hungry intensity, consuming millions of nanites in their path.

Kyle stands transfixed, staring at the inferno. Mesmerized. Heat washes over his face even from this distance. The warehouse buckles and burns before him. Inside, enhancement pills melt into useless slag. Storage units warp and collapse. Steel doors buckle under the onslaught.

Sirens wail in the distance. Kyle takes one last look at the blaze. The orange glow illuminates everything with merciless clarity. There's no going back now. No pretending he's just playing both sides. No hiding behind his parents' reputation or his status as Central City's golden boy.

Claus appears beside him, placing a hand on his shoulder. "The first strike is always the hardest," he says quietly. "The question you must answer now is not whether it was right, but whether you are prepared for what comes next."

Kyle watches the flames reach higher into the night sky. "What does come next?"

Francesca's voice is steel. "War."

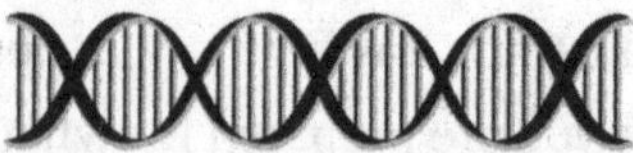

CHAPTER 9

KYLE'S PALM stings as it connects with the practice pad another speedster holds steady. He releases punch after jab after punch after jab, the pent-up anger in his body leaching away with every hiss of breath. Claus keeps an eye on them as he trains with Silver, occasionally barking corrections in his clipped German accent. The gym echoes with the rhythmic slap of flesh against padding, the squeak of feet on mats, the measured breathing of focused athletes. Silver performs a Kata on the other side of the mats.

If only he could do this all day. Every day. No interviews. No nighttime raids. No resistance. Just... peace, karate, and the mats.

"Again," Claus calls from across the room. "Your speed is not your strength, Kyle-kun. Control is."

Kyle resets his stance. He's about to strike when the PA system blares to life.

"Students," the voice of our principal screeches. "Please

stay where you are and do not proceed to homeroom. We have a special announcement coming."

Kyle raises a brow as he stares at the speakers. His guts tell him he knows exactly what this announcement is about.

A walkie-talkie crackles from Claus' gym bag. He holds it to his ear.

"I understand," Claus says into the walkie, pulling at his mustache. He disconnects the call and gestures for them all to follow him toward the wall-mounted monitor at the far end of the gym.

Picking up the remote, Claus thumbs the power button. The whispered conversations fall quiet. Students gather around. Silver is beside him. They share a look. But neither says a word.

The screen comes to life and the presidential seal fills every inch of it.

"Terror attack?" Kyle whispers in Silver's ear, hoping that it is, knowing it's far worse. But they destroyed so many nanites, how can they be rolling out a program now?

Silver shrugs, lost in her own world, her jaw tight, her finger tapping against her thigh.

"Da-da-da-dum..." Jax calls, laughing.

"Shhh." Claus glares at those making noise.

"What is going on?" Kyle mutters under his breath, not quite believing the moment he has been preparing for for months is finally here.

On the monitor, the presidential seal is replaced by a room in the White House. The camera pans to a horde of journalists sitting in temporary seating, their faces tense, jotting notes on smartphones. The bell rings, signaling they should be in homeroom.

"This is bad, isn't it?" Kyle asks, unable to stop the incessant, babbling questions.

"Always," Silver replies, with a knife in her hand he hadn't noticed. Where the hell did she get a thing like that?

President Bear's face fills the screen—the broad, almost ursine features that earned him his nickname long before he took the bear nanite. His eyes gleam red in the studio lights, a side effect of his multiple enhancements.

"This is a national announcement," Bear says, his deep voice reverberating through the silent gym. "All unadjusteds age twelve and over will now be required to take a nanite pill to enhance their abilities."

Kyle's heart stutters. This really is it.

"With threats and competition from overseas, we must do more to further the strength of our country."

Silver stands perfectly still beside him, the only movement the rapid rise and fall of her chest. Kyle watches her throat work as she swallows. Among the clustered group, the handful of other unadjusteds have gone pale, frozen in place like prey waiting to be picked off.

"The nanite representative agency is on its way to every school right now," Bear continues, his red eyes seeming to stare directly at each viewer. "They will assign each eligible unadjusted a ticket number. You are not permitted to leave before you have your ticket."

Kyle's gaze shifts around the gym—to the exits, to the windows, to the vulnerable, terrified faces of the unadjusteds. There's nowhere to run. Not now. Not with what he knows about the government's surveillance capabilities. *Hellhounds.* A person could be torn apart in five seconds flat.

"This ticket will tell you which day within the next two weeks you will be assessed for an appropriate nanite level." Bear's mouth curls into what might be a smile on anyone else. On him, it's a baring of teeth. "You'll notice some of those assessments start today. Nanite reps and soldiers are on their way to each school in every city to aid the process."

Soldiers. Kyle's stomach drops. His father's computer didn't reveal this part of the plan. But he hadn't had long to sniff around.

Kyle glances at Silver, sees not fear but rage burning in her eyes.

Silver stumbles. Claus grabs her. "Breathe, Silver."

"Once this assessment is complete," Bear continues, "we will proceed to residences to evaluate the unadjusted adults. I expect each unadjusted individual to join the strength of the adjusted superbeings."

A boy in the corner lets out a small, choked sound. His parents are both unadjusteds. Everyone knows they've been vocal about their right to remain unmodified. He's seen them at the warehouse.

"Failure to comply will result in *unfortunate circum-stances.*" The threat hangs in the air. "Our country is the most powerful in the world. Your loyalty and patriotism is expect-ed." The President leans forward slightly, his massive frame filling the screen. "But in case you need a reminder of what happens to traitors..."

The image changes.

A woman is being dragged between two guards, her

wrists cuffed behind her back. Despite the poor quality of the footage, there's no mistaking her identity.

Dr. Margaret Melody. Silver's mother.

Kyle hears Silver's sharp intake of breath. Feels her entire body go rigid beside him. He turns just in time to see all the color drain from her face, her silver eyes wide with shock and horror.

"Mom," she whispers, the word barely audible.

The footage continues, showing Margaret being shoved into a windowless van, her head forced down by a guard's heavy hand. The camera zooms in on her face for one brutal moment—enough for everyone to see the resemblance to the girl standing frozen beside him.

"The time for debate is over," Bear concludes as the footage returns to his face. "The time for unity of purpose has arrived. Together, we will become the most advanced, most powerful nation in history."

The screens go dark for a moment, then return to their previous displays as if nothing has happened. The gym remains silent, the announcement hanging in the air like poison gas.

"They can't do this," Kyle whispers.

A few eyes turn in his direction.

Claus shuts off the monitor.

"Can they really do that?" Kyle asks, silently challenging the altereds in the room.

"It's not our place to question the will of the president," Claus says, his voice low.

"Dude, didn't you just set a record?" someone at the back of the group asks Kyle. "The mile, wasn't it?"

"I..." Kyle's mouth gapes open. "I *chose* the speed nanite. But it shouldn't be forced on someone if they don't want it." Although he knew this day was coming, has been preparing for it, the reality leaves him reeling.

"No, it shouldn't be forced on anyone." Silver says, the fury in her voice hard to miss. "So much for living in a democracy."

Kyle faces her. "What are you going to do? You're unadjusted."

She doesn't answer verbally, just shrugs and slides the knife up her sleeve like she's about to start her own personal war.

"I don't want to take a pill," a freshman says. She'd be perfect for a pair of fairy wings. "I lost both my brothers to nanite pills. They're not safe!" She sobs, then runs from the room.

"What's the alternative?" Kyle asks quietly.

"You get arrested," Claus says. "Or detained. You heard the president. He speaks in euphemisms. *Unfortunate circumstances?* You'd be lucky. Just look at Silver's mother."

Everyone stares at Silver.

"Whatcha gonna choose, Silver?" Jax crosses his arms and sneers at Silver. "You've always been on the feisty side. Maybe the light of a firefly?"

Anger flashes through Kyle's veins.

"I can't even believe there are any unadjusteds left," Jax drones on until Kyle gives him a look.

"Twenty percent," Silver snaps.

"Won't take long to improve you all then." Jax cracks his knuckles.

If Jax wasn't a bulk, Kyle would punch him.

Silver backs away, toward the doors, but they burst open before she gets there.

Matt stands in the frame. "Let's go," he says, waving Silver over.

Matt and his plans. Plan A was always keeping Silver safe. But Kyle finds it hard to see her go. Knows how much hangs on her.

"Silver, you don't have to leave. Just wait. They can't do this. You'll see." Kyle places a hand on her arm.

Without warning, she buckles over.

Kyle removes his hand. "Silver?"

She snatches a breath. Then another.

Kyle frowns. "Dude, what happened? Are you okay?"

She musters a smile. "It wasn't you. Just a panic attack. I get them sometimes." Then she turns and runs.

Kyle watches her and Matt dash out the wide doors. And then they're gone. He glances back at the cluster of students. Jax and another bulk are messing around. A couple of the unadjusteds are backing toward the windows. Claus gives him a solemn nod. It's time to move.

Without a plan or any goodbyes, Kyle bursts out of the doors. In the hallway, it's chaos. The fluorescent lights flicker overhead, casting the frenetic crowd in stuttered motion like frames of old film. Someone knocks over a water cooler, sending it crashing to the floor. Water spills across the linoleum, making people slip. The fire alarm and sprinklers go off.

Kyle leaps over a spreading puddle, maintaining his speed. The world blurs around him. He slips through a maintenance door, down a service corridor, and emerges near the science wing where more students huddle in terrified clusters. NanoTech reps are already there, scanning IDs, separating enhanced from unadjusted. Kyle doesn't slow down. Can't slow down. If he stops, if he thinks about what's happening, he might never start moving again.

He bursts through the emergency exit at the back of the building, ignoring the alarm that wails in his wake. Outside, the scene that greets him freezes his blood. The parking lot has become a sorting ground. Students are lined up against the wall—unadjusteds only, hands on their heads, guarded by soldiers with pulse rifles. A girl tries to run. A rifle butt catches her in the stomach, doubling her over.

Kyle ducks behind a dumpster, bile rising in his throat. This isn't enhancement. This is a roundup. This is everything the resistance feared.

Two bulks in tactical gear haul a struggling boy toward a waiting van. The boy screams for his parents, for help, for anyone. No one moves. No one can. The bulks throw him inside like cargo.

Kyle swallows, forcing the nausea down. He can't help them, not directly. Not now. His value is in getting to the cave. In ending this.

He maps a route in his head—across the football field, through the maintenance gate, down the service road that runs behind the commercial district. No main streets. No cameras. No patrols.

Taking a deep breath, Kyle activates his speed. He moves past the soldiers, their turning heads captured in freeze-frame like grotesque statues. Past students with tears tracking down immobile faces. Past a NanoTech rep consulting a tablet with Kyle's own face displayed prominently among others.

He hits the main street three blocks from school and the chaos multiplies. Cars abandoned in traffic jams. People fleeing on foot. Bulk soldiers in formation, herding unadjusteds toward buses that will take them off to God knows where. He snatches words like "compound" and "processing center" as he speeds by. They've been planning this. He knew so much, but there was so much more he was ignorant of.

A man breaks from a group, trying to reach a woman being loaded into a different transport vehicle. A bulk catches him easily, massive fist connecting with flesh. The man crumples. No warning. No hesitation. Just violence.

Kyle ducks into an alley. He moves in bursts of speed, conserving energy, staying in shadows whenever possible. Twice he has to freeze as patrol drones sweep overhead, their sensors searching for unregistered movement. The third time, he doesn't spot the drone until it's directly above him, red sensor eye swiveling toward his position.

Kyle doesn't think. He grabs a loose brick from the crumbling wall beside him and hurls it. The brick connects with the drone's stabilizer. The machine spirals down, crashing into a dumpster with a satisfying crunch of metal and circuits. No time to celebrate. Kyle runs.

The suburbs are quieter but no less tense. Curtains drawn. Doors locked. The occasional bulk patrol moving house to house, checking registrations. Kyle slips between properties, vaulting fences and skirting hedges. His family's neighborhood rises ahead—pristine lawns, elegant facades, the homes of Central City's elite. The homes of those who created this nightmare.

His house sits dark and silent at the end of the cul-de-sac. No cars in the driveway. No lights in the windows. His parents are out, probably helping President Bear sell this atrocity to the public. Probably crafting the message that will make imprisonment sound like progress.

Kyle lets himself in through the back door, disabling the security system. He takes the stairs two at a time, moving to his bedroom. The bag is where he left it, tucked into the false bottom of his closet beneath winter clothes he rarely wears. He pulls it out, checks the contents: basic first aid supplies, a burner phone with offline maps, clothes without identifying markers, cash, a fake ID Matt helped him create, protein bars, water purification tablets. The necessities of a life on the run.

He adds more protein bars from his sports bag, a refillable water bottle. Hesitates, then glances at the photo of his parents from his nightstand. The thought of them brings a wave of grief so sudden and intense that Kyle has to sit on the edge of his bed, the room spinning around him. These are his parents. The people who raised him, who taught him to ride a bike, who celebrated his achievements, who held him when he cried. And now they're strangers. Worse than strangers —enemies.

He remembers his mother's smile when she first suggested the speed nanite. His father's pride when Kyle broke his first record. Were they grooming him even then? Was it always leading to this moment, to becoming a weapon against people like Silver?

"I'm sorry," he whispers to the empty room. "I can't be who you want me to be."

He tucks the photo into his bag and zips it closed. As he turns to leave, his gaze catches on the Jacob Shea digi-posters that still adorn his walls. He never did take them down. He wonders if perhaps Jacob faced the same dilemmas as him. The martial arts champion who inspired him for so long now seems like a caricature—enhanced strength, enhanced speed, enhanced precision, all packaged and sold as aspiration rather than coercion.

Kyle puts a boot through the screens, shattering them. He won't be another poster boy. He won't sell lies to terrified kids.

Downstairs, he raids the pantry one last time, grabbing anything non-perishable that will fit in his bag. At the front door, he pauses. Looks back at the home that sheltered him while others wore cuffs and hid in warehouses. Part of him wants to leave a note. To explain. To apologize. To rage. But what could he possibly say that would matter? His parents made their choice long ago.

Kyle adjusts the bag on his shoulder and steps outside. The sun is high, painting Central City in fire. He orients himself toward the Great Woods, toward the cave.

Then he runs, faster than he's ever run before, leaving the golden boy behind. Forever.

CHAPTER 10

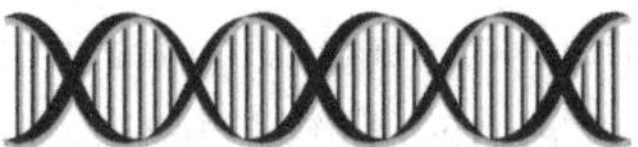

Kyle weaves through the crowded streets, his feet going faster than his brain can take everything in.

The city center has become a war zone in a few short hours—checkpoints at every major intersection, drones humming overhead in tight formation, bulks in tactical gear herding frightened unadjusteds into armored buses.

A woman stumbles into him, eyes wild with panic. "They took my son," she whispers, fingers digging into his arm. "Right from school. Said his profile was so low he didn't deserve a nanite. They took him. I don't know where—"

Kyle gently extricates himself, throat tight. "I'm sorry," he says. There is nothing he can do.

A massive screen that normally blasts advertisements for the latest nanites suddenly flickers to life. Kyle throws a look over his shoulder. Sees another digi-board doing the same down the street. Every display in the plaza—the curved billboards wrapping around skyscrapers to the personal devices in people's hands—all switch to the same image: the presidential seal.

Kyle freezes mid-step. The crowd around him slows, eyes lifting to the nearest screen.

His father's face fills the display. He no longer recognizes it. His father wears the dark blue suit reserved for important announcements, the NanoTech pin gleaming on his lapel.

"Citizens of Central City," his father begins, voice echoing across the plaza from a dozen speakers. "The future waits for no one. Progress demands sacrifice. Even our own children must evolve or be left behind."

The words hit Kyle like a physical blow. *His own children.* His father is talking about him. About all of them. About sacrificing an entire generation to Bear's vision.

"The mandatory enhancement program is proceeding smoothly," his father continues, wearing the reassuring smile he practiced in the mirror at home. "Those who embrace progress will find their place in our new society. Those who resist..." He pauses, allowing the threat to hang unspoken.

On-screen, his father stands straighter, pride radiating from his perfect posture. "My own son has demonstrated the benefits of enhancement since childhood. Today, he continues to inspire others with his exceptional abilities."

Kyle's stomach twists. They don't know he's gone yet. They're still using him as propaganda. His face appears in the corner of the screen.

"All parents must make this choice for the greater good," his father says. "Our children's potential is our nation's future."

Kyle backs away from the crowd, bile rising in his throat.

His father sold him. Sold everyone. And for what? Position? Power? Some twisted vision of the future where humanity no longer exists?

A low, rumbling growl cuts through his thoughts. An unnatural sound that belongs to no ordinary animal. His blood goes cold.

Hellhounds.

He spots them rounding the corner—three massive beasts with glossy black hides rippling over unnatural muscle. Their eyes glow sickly yellow, jaws lined with teeth too numerous, too sharp. Steam rises from their nostrils as they strain against reinforced leashes, heads swinging from side to side, scenting.

Their handlers scan the crowd, checking faces against tablets. Looking for unadjusteds. Looking for runners.

Looking for him?

Kyle doesn't wait to find out. He ducks into an alley. Once out of direct sight, he activates his speed.

The world slows around him. His legs pump, muscles burning. The ground blurs beneath his feet as he cuts through service corridors, around dumpsters, past the backs of restaurants where kitchen staff freeze as he passes.

Each breath tears at his lungs. Sweat soaks through his shirt, plastering it to his back. He's been running for hours—from school to home to here—and even with his enhancements, fatigue is setting in.

Kyle emerges onto a wider street and skids to a stop, sneakers scraping against concrete. Directly ahead, blocking his path, stands a squad of Youth Enforcers in matching black uniforms with red armbands. And at their center, taller than the others—Jax.

Kyle's former friend spots him instantly, eyes narrowing in recognition. An arrogant smile spreads across Jax's face.

"Kyle Lewis," Jax calls out, voice echoing off concrete. "Well, well, well."

Kyle straightens, forcing his breathing to steady. "Hey, Jax. Nice outfit. Does it come with a personality, or is that extra?"

The smile falters. Jax takes a step forward, his enhanced frame casting a long shadow in the searchlights that sweep periodically across the street. "President Bear has personally requested your presence. Special training program for elite enhanced youth." He holds out a hand. "Come on, man. Don't make this difficult. You're one of us."

"One of *you?*" Kyle gestures to the squad, their faces eager and cruel beneath the identical caps. "Since when did *one of us* mean hunting people down for refusing pills?"

Jax's jaw tightens. "They're resisting progress. We're securing the future." He sounds like a propaganda broadcast. Maybe he believes it. Maybe he needs to.

"I saw what your *future* looks like." Kyle's voice drops. "Kids deemed too unworthy of enhancement loaded into vans. People beaten for asking questions." He shakes his head. "Dude, that's not progress. That's control."

Something flickers in Jax's eyes—doubt, maybe, or recognition. But it vanishes as quickly as it came.

"Last chance, Kyle. Come willingly." Jax's fingers flex at his sides. "For old times' sake."

Kyle meets his gaze. "I'm already gone."

He moves before the last word leaves his mouth, his speed carrying him directly toward the squad. They reach for him, fingers grasping at empty air as he cuts between them, under Jax's outstretched arm, and toward the building behind.

"Stop him!" Jax roars.

Kyle leaps, catching the bottom rung of a fire escape. His muscles scream as he hauls himself up, metal rattling beneath his weight. A hand grabs his ankle. Kyle kicks free, scrambling higher.

The fire escape groans as Jax jumps after him. Kyle climbs faster. He reaches the rooftop and sprints across it, leaping the narrow gap to the next building.

Behind him, Jax lands heavily on the rooftop, concrete cracking under the impact. "You can't run forever, Kyle!" he shouts. "There's nowhere to go!"

Kyle doesn't look back. He runs, feet pounding across tar and gravel, jumping from building to building. He feels a bit like a superhero, but with burning lungs and trembling legs. Do superheroes get burning lungs and trembling legs?

He shakes the unnecessary thoughts out of his head and pushes on. The city spreads below him—streets sectioned by checkpoints, alleys prowled by hellhounds, plazas filled with screens showing his father's face. Every block, every corner a dead end.

"Nowhere to go," Jax had said.

But Kyle knows better. He's heading somewhere. Somewhere they haven't found. Somewhere they won't ever find.

The Great Woods wait on the horizon. And beyond that, the cave. Matt. Francesca. The resistance.

Home.

After he loses Jax, Kyle drops into a narrow gap between warehouses on the edge of the city. He braces himself against concrete walls on either side, forcing air into his overused lungs. His body can't take much more. He needs rest, water, something to quiet the growl in his stomach. Hunger claws at him, reminding him that enhanced metabolism comes with a price. The shadows lengthen as evening settles over the city, painting everything in blues and grays. Safer now. Darker. But not safe enough.

The sound of a cough catches his attention. Then rustling. Then whispers.

"Shut up, they'll hear us."

"I can't stop coughing. It's the tear gas."

"Then cover your mouth."

Kyle edges forward, moving silently past overflowing trash bins and discarded packaging. Behind a large industrial dumpster, huddled in the narrow space between metal and brick wall, he finds them—five teenagers, none older than him. Unadjusteds.

Their clothes are torn and filthy, smeared with dirt and what looks like dried blood. A boy clutches his arm to his chest, the wrist bent at an unnatural angle. Another rocks back and forth, eyes vacant, a shock victim if Kyle's ever seen one. A girl with dark circles under her eyes keeps glancing toward the street, her entire body coiled tight like a spring. Two others—a boy and a girl—press together for warmth, both shivering despite the mild evening air.

The girl nearest the edge spots Kyle first. Her face is a constellation of bruises, purple and yellow spreading across her left cheek and eye. She scrambles back, hissing a warning to the others.

"Wait," Kyle says, keeping his voice low. He raises his hands, showing he's unarmed. "I'm not with them."

"Bullshit," spits the boy with the broken wrist. "You're Kyle Lewis."

"I am," he says. "But I'm helping the resistance."

The group exchanges glances, suspicion all over their faces.

"Prove it," says the bruised girl.

Kyle crouches, making himself smaller, less threatening. "I know where you can go. Somewhere safe. Outside the city." He glances over his shoulder, checking for patrols. "But we don't have much time. You need to move tonight, before they expand the search grid."

The shock victim stops rocking, focusing on Kyle for the first time. "What search grid?"

"They're going section by section. Hellhounds, drones, thermal scans." Kyle swallows. "They're prioritizing schools and youth centers first. Gathering the easy targets."

The huddling pair separate slightly. "Why would you help us?" the girl asks.

"Because I can." Kyle reaches into his pocket, pulls out a crumpled napkin, the only paper he has. "Listen carefully. I'm only going to say this once."

He smooths the paper against his knee, fishing a pen from his jacket. "You need to get to Westbrook Station. Not the main entrance—there's a service door on the south side, behind the maintenance shed." He sketches a crude map. "The lock is broken if you push hard enough. Inside, follow the old service tunnel. It's been abandoned since they built the new line."

The teens lean forward, watching his pen mark the route.

"The tunnel runs for about three miles. Parts of it are flooded, but never more than knee-deep. After the third junction, look for a maintenance shaft on the left." He circles a spot on the map. "The ladder leads up to a drainage ditch just inside the forest edge."

"The Great Woods?" The bruised girl's voice drops to a whisper.

Kyle nods. "Once you're in the trees, head east until you get to these coordinates and find three pines growing in a triangle formation." His pen marks an X. "The cave entrance is hidden behind them, down in a small valley. There are people there who will help you."

"What about patrols?" asks the boy with the broken wrist, now leaning forward despite his pain. "Those dogs...?"

"Stick to the tunnel until you reach the woods. The water will mask your scent from the hellhounds." Kyle taps the map. "Avoid open spaces, even in the forest. Drones run perimeter sweeps every thirty minutes, but they rarely penetrate more than half a mile into the tree line."

"How do we know this isn't a trap?" The shock victim has come back to himself enough to voice the question they're all thinking.

Kyle meets his gaze steadily. "You don't. But staying here is certain capture."

He folds the map carefully, pressing it into the bruised girl's hand. She seems the strongest, the most focused.

"Why are you helping us?" she asks, fingers closing around the paper. "You're one of them. Enhanced. Safe."

The question hits harder than it should. "Because I helped build the system that's hunting you," he says finally. The words taste like ash. "My father works directly for President Bear. My mother runs propaganda campaigns. And I'm their poster child for successful enhancement." He looks away. "I can't undo what they've done. But I can try to help fix it."

Silence falls between them. Kyle reaches into his pack, pulls out his emergency rations—protein bars, water purification tablets, a small first aid kit.

"Take these. There's food and water in the cave, but you'll need something for the journey."

The bruised girl accepts the supplies, her eyes never leaving his face. "Thank you."

Kyle nods, rises to his feet. "Leave as soon as it's fully dark. Stay together." He adjusts his pack. "And when you reach the cave, ask for me. Or if I'm not there." He hides a dry swallow. "Tell them I sent you."

"You're not coming with us?" asks the boy with the broken wrist.

Kyle shakes his head. "I can cover more ground alone. And I have other stops to make." He doesn't elaborate. Doesn't tell them he's planning to check other hiding spots, other alleys unadjusteds are known to gather.

"Good luck," he says, already backing toward the alley entrance.

The bruised girl clutches the map tighter. "You too."

Kyle slips away, running through the night, listening out

for stranded unadjusteds. After he finds five other groups and gives them all directions, he makes his way toward the woods. His legs give out three times before he reaches the tree line. By the time the concrete turns to soil and the streetlights fade behind him, his body moves on autopilot—one foot, then the other, a rhythm as mindless as breathing. The Great Woods rise around him. No cameras here. No drones. Yet. Hellhounds? Probably. He's damn glad he can outrun them. But he's exhausted and not sure how much longer he can hold his speed.

Kyle slows to a jog as he pushes deeper. The air tastes different here—clean, sharp with pine resin and loamy earth. No chemical tang of exhaust or the metallic aftertaste of city life.

Stars peek through gaps in the canopy, more than he's ever seen from Central City's light-polluted skies. Kyle navigates by their faint glow, moving west through the underbrush, checking landmarks he memorized during previous excursions. A lightning-struck oak. A stream that bends like a question mark. A rock formation resembling a rabbit.

Hours pass. Then a night. And another day. Pain creeps in—muscles screaming, joints aching. Still, he pushes forward. The valley should be just ahead. The stand of pines. The hidden entrance.

When Kyle finally spots the three pines growing in a triangle formation, he nearly weeps with relief. He stumbles down the gentle slope into the small valley. A door in the mouth of the cave is firmly shut, half-concealed by underbrush, exactly as they left it.

Kyle squeezes through the narrow opening, shuffles along

the passageway, and finds himself in the main chamber. Their supplies remain untouched on the other side of the massive area—lanterns, sleeping bags, canned food, water purification tablets.

He grabs a sleeping bag, heads down another passage until he finds the little alcoves designated for private areas, and collapses, not bothering to remove his shoes. The last thought before unconsciousness claims him is simple: *I made it.*

Kyle wakes to the sound of a steady drip of water. His body feels leaden, muscles stiff from overexertion and the cold cave floor. According to his watch, he's slept for fifteen hours straight.

He forces himself up, ignoring the protests of his aching limbs. He has no idea when the others will arrive. *If* they'll arrive.

Kyle turns on the connected lanterns Matt wired up. Immediately, a soft glow spreads through the cave, making him feel not quite so alone. Then he checks the filtration system at the underground lake.

A couple of days pass. Kyle worries about Matt and Francesca and Claus. It's a long hike and he's not expecting them to appear until the end of the week... But still... Did they make it out of the city? And what about those groups of teenagers he gave directions to? He shakes his head. He found getting here tough and he has enhanced speed. What if they all came across hellhounds, or the bulk army or were detained in processing centers?

And what the hell are they going to do to the unadjusteds in the processing centers? Maybe the nanite program was all a ruse. Maybe all President Bear wanted to do was round up the unadjusteds and stick them somewhere out of the way. Delete them from existence.

The thought makes Kyle's stomach roil.

Kyle ventures out only to set simple snares for rabbits and gather edible plants he recognizes from Claus' wilderness training. He establishes routines. Checks the entrance every two hours. Maintains a small fire in a chamber with proper ventilation. Keeps watch.

On the fourth day, as dusk settles over the forest, Kyle hears movement outside the cave entrance. He grabs the taser they stashed before and presses himself against the wall beside the opening.

"Kyle?" Matt's voice echoes from outside. "It's us."

Relief floods through him. "Here," Kyle calls back, lowering the weapon.

Matt enters first, his sandy hair dirty and disheveled, face streaked with grime. Behind him are Francesca and Claus. Claus with a new limp and a story of a shootout. Then there's Matt's family and a girl with bright green macaw wings. And behind her is a clump of six teenagers—thin, frightened, but alive.

"Made it," Matt says simply, dropping his pack. He clasps Kyle's shoulder briefly. "Barely."

Kyle notices that one of Matt's sisters is missing, but he's too afraid to voice the question.

Francesca organizes the newcomers, directing them to sleeping areas and rummaging through the food supplies. No one had time to grab much. "Central City's locked down tight," she tells Kyle, voice low. "Checkpoints at every exit.

Drone sweeps every thirty minutes. We had to go north through the industrial zone, then circle back."

"Any sign of Silver?" Kyle asks.

Matt shakes his head. "I gave her directions. It'll be a few days before we see her and her father."

Kyle nods, swallowing his disappointment. If anyone can get them out of his mess, it's Dr. Rufus Melody.

"Good work, Kyle-kun," Claus says. "You have done well."

Coming from Claus, it's high praise.

"News from the city is not good," Claus continues.

"Casualties?" Kyle asks.

Claus' face tightens. "Many. On both sides."

"And alts going nuts in the streets," Matt adds. "Murdering each other. Murdering anyone."

"Why?" Kyle asks.

Matt shrugs. "Didn't hang around long enough to find out. But Rufus mentioned something about a God-Factor. That alts who've taken multiple nanites need to be around unadjusteds to keep them psychologically grounded because they've lost so much of their human DNA. It was something he wasn't allowed to test."

"Typical," Kyle mutters, wondering how much his father was involved with that decision.

As evening approaches, two more figures slip through the cave entrance—Erica, her butterfly wings folded tightly against her back, and Addison, an incredibly tall female with long auburn hair. Kyle notes the throwing stars strapped to a band on her wrist. She could be handy. And it's nice to have some other altereds here. To know he's not the only one with enhancements who is unhappy with current leadership.

"Home sweet hole in the ground," Erica says, her attempt at sarcasm undermined by the visible relief in her face. "Please tell me someone packed decent food."

Beside her, Addison remains quiet, her gaze sweeping the cave's interior.

Erica drops her pack on the ground. "So many checkpoints and hellhounds and drones—"

"It was rough," Addison says.

By nightfall, their numbers have grown to twenty-three. Relieved and hopeful voices echo off limestone walls. The natural chimneys steam as the smell of pasta fills the cave. Matt's radio equipment hums with static as he attempts to establish contact with other resistance cells.

Kyle pokes through the food supplies after dinner. People are on the verge of starving. And they're going to need food if they want to fight.

"We need more of everything," Francesca says to him. "All those runs felt like a different world. Some kind of dream. But now..." she shakes her head.

Kyle knows exactly how she's feeling. They all hoped they wouldn't need this hideout. But here they are.

"Paige, the girl with green wings, says she's happy to go on supply runs," Francesca says. "You two would make a good team."

Kyle nods. "We'll start tomorrow."

"There are ID cards," Francesca says. "If you get stopped without one, you might be detained."

"I'll come up with a story," Kyle replies, rubbing the back of his neck. "I am Kyle Lewis, after all."

Francesca gives him a rare smile and claps his shoulder. "You're a good kid."

His ears heat with the praise. "You're a good teacher."

Francesca's smile turns to a laugh.

The next morning, in the comms room, Kyle spreads a map across a portable table, weighing down the corners with small stones. He traces the route with his finger—from the cave through the densest part of the Great Woods, then along the eastern ridge where the tree cover provides protection from aerial surveillance, and finally down to the small town of Pinecrest. Six miles as the crow flies. Ten if they stick to cover. A five-hour journey for normal humans. For him, with his speed? Forty minutes, maybe. For Paige, with her wings? Unknown.

"We have three weeks of food," Paige says, kneeling beside him. Her emerald wings folded neatly against her back, occasional feathers catching the light when she shifts position. "And the medical kits are almost empty."

Kyle nods, studying the inventory list Francesca compiled. " So many are arriving injured. We need more antibiotics. Bandages. Pain meds." He rubs his temple. "Everything, basically."

"Pinecrest has a pharmacy and a grocery store," Paige points to the town on the map. "But they'll be roadblocks."

"Which is why we go in fast, get what we need, and get out faster." Kyle glances at her wings. "How long can you stay airborne?"

Paige stretches one wing. "All day if I'm just gliding. Less if I have to do a lot of flapping." She flexes the wing, demonstrating the powerful muscles. "I've never tried carrying much weight."

"You can be our eyes," Kyle says. "Scout ahead, warn us about patrols." He traces a circle above Pinecrest on the map. "If you stay high enough, they won't spot you against the night sky."

Paige nods, studying the route. "What about your speed? How long can you maintain it?"

Kyle checks his watch, calculating. "At full sprint, maybe an hour before I'm completely drained. Longer if I pace myself. But I'll need to conserve energy for the return trip. Especially if we're carrying supplies."

"Matt said we could take the jeep to the edge of town."

Kyle nods. "That'll help."

Across the cave, Matt calibrates the radio equipment while Francesca organizes the unadjusteds into work groups. Claus trains some in basic self-defense moves. Their community grows more organized by the hour, but their needs grow just as quickly.

"We need to prioritize," Kyle says, turning to their inventory list. "Medicine first. Food second."

Paige points to a spot on the map. "There's a stream here where we can set up fishing lines. And these hills have wild berries in season." She tucks a strand of dark hair behind her ear.

"That's good thinking," Kyle says. "We should mark foraging spots for future runs."

They spend the next hour planning contingencies, escape routes, meeting points if they get separated.

Matt joins them as they pack small backpacks. "We

received a transmission from another resistance cell near the West Coast," he says. "Bear's forces are... everywhere. Entire towns are being locked down for *processing*."

Kyle's stomach drops. "It's everywhere?"

"As we feared." Matt's eyes are hard. "You two need to be very, very careful. If you can manage to grab an approved nanite ID card somewhere, I can see if I can duplicate them. But it's not worth your life..."

"I'm on it," Kyle says.

Matt nods, then hands them each a small device no bigger than a thumbnail. "Communication pins. Short range, encrypted. Press twice to send an alert, three times for emergency extraction."

"Extraction by who?" Paige asks, securing the pin to her collar.

Matt's mouth quirks. "Still working on that part. But at least we'll know you're in trouble."

Kyle checks his watch—7:42 PM. Sunset. The safest time to move, when human vision is compromised but before the night patrols begin thermal scanning.

"Time to go," he says, shouldering his pack.

Francesca approaches. "No risks. No heroes. Just in and out." She hands Kyle a small taser.

Kyle tucks the weapon into his waistband, hidden beneath his T-shirt. The weight of it sits uncomfortably against his spine. Outside of the mats, Kyle has never hurt anyone. Not on purpose.

They make their way through the cave's winding passages toward the entrance, followed by the hushed good wishes of the others. At the narrow opening, Kyle pauses, listening for unusual sounds. Nothing but forest noise—wind in leaves, distant owl calls, the soft rustling of nocturnal creatures.

"Clear," he whispers.

They slip out into the gathering darkness, the last purple light of dusk fading from the western sky. The air smells of pine and damp earth, cooler now as night approaches. Kyle orients himself using the stars emerging overhead, then points east.

"We follow the ridge for the first mile," he says. "Stay under the canopy until we reach the overlook. Then we can grab the jeep for a stretch."

Paige nods, wings half-extended in readiness. "I'll fly ahead in short bursts. Three chirps means danger, two means all clear."

The forest enfolds them as they move forward, pine needles cushioning their footsteps. Kyle adjusts his pace to match Paige's, resisting the urge to activate his speed.

Occasionally, Paige launches herself upward through gaps in the canopy to check their surroundings. Each time she returns with a double chirp—all clear—landing gracefully beside him before they continue.

KYLE ADJUSTS the woman's stance. "Weight on your back foot," he says. "When a bulk comes at you, you don't meet force with force."

He presses lightly on her shoulder, angling her body away from the imaginary attacker. Around him, the small chamber echoes with the rhythmic thud of feet against stone and the sharp exhales of exhausted resistance members. Many of them still injured.

"Now pivot," Kyle continues, demonstrating the move at half-speed. "Use their momentum. Let them commit." He steps forward, playing the role of attacker, his movements deliberately slowed.

Across the chamber, Claus circles another group, adjusting to his limp and the wound he refuses to let anyone tend. "The bulk will expect you to run," he tells them. "This is your advantage."

The fighters nod wearily. It will take years to train them into elite fighting machines. They don't have years. But they do have determination. And combined with grit, that goes a long way.

"Again," Claus commands, clapping his hands once. "From the beginning. Five sequences."

Kyle moves through the line, correcting grips, adjusting stances, offering quiet encouragement. Their progress over the past week has been remarkable—but that's what a mixture of focus and rage will do for you.

In the far corner, away from the others, Hal works alone. The sandbags groan under his massive hands as he lifts them, muscles rippling beneath skin that's been reinforced by the bulk nanite. Eight feet tall and nearly as wide, he dwarfs everyone in the cave. Kyle pauses to watch him. There's something incongruous about Hal's size and the careful, almost delicate way he handles the training equipment.

"Any news from your buddy? Joe, was it?" Kyle asks, approaching the giant.

Hal lowers the sandbag, short, dark hair flinging beads of sweat as he shakes his head. "Not yet. But he'll find a way. Joe always does."

"Bulks on our side will be super helpful."

"Can't argue with that."

"Can't wait to have a go at the training course you and Claus set up. Gonna break some records, dude."

Hal chuckles and lays a hand on his shoulder. "As soon as we get the all-clear from Matt and we can be sure there aren't any helicopters in the area. Bet I can give you a run for your money."

Kyle grins. "You're on."

He returns to the main group, where Claus has paired

fighters for defensive drills. Kyle slips into position opposite a young man with anxious eyes. Hell, they all have anxious eyes. They've all lost something on the way here. They all have something to fight for.

They move through the sequence—attack, block, counter, reset. Kyle keeps his speed in check, focusing on form rather than power.

"Good," Claus says, moving between the pairs. "Remember what you learn here. When the time comes, your body must know before your mind."

Raised voices echoing down the passageway break their rhythm. Everyone freezes, heads turning toward the tunnel. In the days since Bear's announcement, they've nearly doubled their numbers. And they're still waiting for the day when they are found.

Kyle catches Claus' eye. The older man nods once.

Kyle doesn't hesitate. He's through the tunnel entrance before the others have lowered their practice weapons. The tunnel walls blur past, lit intermittently by the lanterns. The main chamber looms ahead, the space opening up from narrow passage to cavernous hall.

He enters at full speed, taking in the scene in fractions of a second: Matt standing near the entrance passageway. Francesca stepping forward from the supply area, hand hovering near the taser at her hip. Paige floating near the ceiling with her wings spread.

Kyle spots the new bulk. His pores prickle with tension. Then he sees Silver.

His breath catches. He drops out of his enhanced speed so suddenly that he stumbles.

Silver.

She made it.

She leans against the limestone wall, dark hair matted with sweat and what might be blood, silver eyes dulled with exhaustion. Her clothes are torn and muddied, her ankle cuff nowhere to be seen. She's alive. She's here.

Kyle throws his arms around her shoulders. "Silver!"

She offers a weak smile. "Hi, Kyle," she says. "If we've got you here, we'll be taking down Bear before we know it."

Kyle grins and punches the air, then winces and adds, "Sorry about hurting you in the gym the other day."

Silver dismisses him with a wave. Her smile fades as she wipes a weary hand over her face. The bulk shifts beside her, a protective stance, his massive frame creating a barrier between her and the rest of the chamber. Matt hovers on her other side.

"How'd you get here?" Kyle asks. "Matt said you and your dad—"

"My dad's been captured," Silver says, the words falling like stones. "Hellhound attack. Army grabbed him."

The cave goes silent. This is *not* good news. Understatement of the century. If the whispers are true, Dr. Rufus Melody was going to help them find a cure of some kind. Without him...

"But you got away," Kyle says.

Silver nods, raking a hand through her tangles. "Joe saved me." She looks at the bulk.

"You saved me too," the bulk says. Kyle doesn't miss the look in his eyes. Kyle looks at Matt. He's wearing the same loved-up look. Uh-oh.

"How did they find you?" Francesca asks, offering a water canteen.

Silver accepts the water, drinking deeply before answering. "Hellhounds tracked our scent. His leg... we need to get him back."

"And we will," Francesca says. "But first you need rest."

"They'll use him," Silver says, eyes closing briefly. "To figure out why all the alts went cray-cray. No offense." She adds with a fragile smile. "And Bear will force him to develop new enhancements. More powerful ones."

That statement chills Kyle to the bone. What could be worse than a hellhound? He doesn't want to know.

Joe shifts his weight, drawing Kyle's attention. "We should get her somewhere to rest," the bulk says, his brown eyes warm with concern. "She's been through hell."

"I'm fine," Silver protests, but her body betrays her as her knee buckles. Joe catches her with surprising gentleness for hands so large.

"I'll show you where," Matt says.

Joe nods, cradling Silver to his side. She doesn't protest, which tells Kyle more about her condition than any words could.

With Matt leading the way, Joe guides Silver toward the tunnel that goes to the sleeping alcoves.

Kyle grabs a quick dinner with Paige, and then Matt is back, giving him that secret nod. They gather in a private corner, a niche sheltered from view by a particularly large stalagmite and the shadows cast by the lantern light.

"What is it?" Kyle asks.

Matt leans against the cool stone, his bright blue eyes serious. Man, they're always serious. "President Bear has placed a one-million-dollar bounty on Silver's head for *safe return.*"

"Holy shit! A million? That's—"

"More money than most people will see in a lifetime," Matt finishes. "Especially unadjusteds who can't get work anymore. Or who might want an exchange for immunity."

Kyle's eyes dart toward the gathered crowd in the main chamber. A million dollars. Enough to change someone's life. Enough to buy a new identity, a ticket out of the country, safety for a family.

Enough to buy betrayal.

"Who knows she's here?" he asks.

"Too many," Matt admits. "We've had new people arriving daily. From what I can tell, they're all legitimate refugees, but..." He doesn't finish the thought. Doesn't need to.

Kyle scans the people again, cataloging faces. The woman he was training earlier, her eyes hollow with recent trauma. The boy with the broken wrist he found hiding in an alley. Paige, who flew cover for him on their supply run. Hal, who's close to the new bulk. Faces he knows. Faces he doesn't.

Any of them could be the one.

"We need to move her," Kyle says. "Set up a separate location. Just a few of us who know."

Matt shakes his head. "It's more dangerous to run two locations. Not to mention the supply issues. Better to keep her here, where we have numbers and security protocols." He runs a hand through his sandy hair. "But we watch everyone."

Kyle nods. Trust no one. Watch everyone.

"It's unlikely someone here will betray her," Matt says.

"They've all been through so much. Lost too much. They want revenge as much as you and me."

"But we can't take any chances."

"Exactly."

"I'll spend more time outside," he says. "My speed gives me an advantage if someone tries something."

"Good," Matt says. "I'll work with Francesca to set up a team of people we can trust."

Kyle thinks of his parents, of how completely he trusted them once. Of how wrong he was. "Is there anyone we trust absolutely anymore?"

Matt doesn't answer. The silence stretches between them, filled with the distant sounds of the cave—water dripping, voices murmuring, a trickle of laughter. Finally, he claps Kyle on the shoulder.

"Get some rest when you can," Matt says. "We're going to need everyone at their best."

Kyle watches him go, then turns back to the main chamber. Somewhere among the gathering, possibly, is someone calculating the value of a million dollars.

Kyle takes a deep breath. Training fighters against a bulk army is hard enough. But now? With Silver here and any number of traitors among them... Kyle doesn't know what to think.

It doesn't matter, he tells himself. Here, they have hope, and that is their biggest weapon.

The End

. . .

If you want to know what happens to Kyle once he meets up with Silver and team, don't forget to check out *The Unadjusteds*:

https://geni.us/Theunadjusteds

Read on for a sneak peek of the next origin story,
Jacob Shea.

If you want to experience more of my books, do join my Facebook readers group where you can chat to other readers and discuss my books, as well as anything else you are reading. I am very active in this group, and you can expect book jokes, puzzles, riddles, quizzes, giveaways, the opportunity to name characters, as well as secret information about what I'm working on, cover reveals and so much more!

Just click here: https://www.facebook.com/groups/840324970233576

Read on for a sneak peek of the next origin story,
Jacob Shea.

FREEBIE

If you'd like to read the next book in the series for FREE, please sign up to my newsletter at

https://www.marisanoelle.com/subscribe/

Don't forget there are 10 more companion novellas in the series:
Silver Melody
Matt Lawson
Joe Rucker
Erica Swiftfield
Paige Starling
Hal Small
Jacob Shea
Sawyer Watson
Addison Shields
President Bear

Turn the page for a sneak peek of the next origin story,
Jacob Shea.

JACOB SHEA

An Unadjusteds Story

MARISA NOELLE

They promised him trophies.

They never warned him what he'd lose to stay on top.

Thirteen-year-old Jacob Shea scrubs dojo floors while his mother works herself to exhaustion just to keep them fed. When a fallen martial arts master offers him a chance at greatness, Jacob swallows his doubts—and a nanite that changes everything. Faster. Stronger. Sharper. For the first time, the world sees him.

But glory comes with a cost. Each victory feeds the greed of his mentor and drags Jacob further from the boy his mother raised. By seventeen, his body is breaking down, his future crumbling, and the regime that created the nanites has begun rounding up those who resist. When soldiers tear his mother away, Jacob's power is no longer a gift—it's all he has left.

In a world obsessed with perfection, how far will one boy go to prove his humanity?

Jacob follows his mother through the dojo's doors as the sun breaks over the rooftops. There are no students yet. Just him, his mother, and hours of work before the first class begins.

His mom unlocks the supply closet. Jacob watches her dump powdered soap into wooden buckets, the water turning milky white as she stirs it with a gloved hand. He grabs a mop without being asked. Two weeks into the summer break and he knows the routine. Not that he likes is. He'd rather be one of the students flipping people on the mats.

"Corner-to-corner today," his mom says, her voice still thick from sleep. "Master Han has the regional qualifiers coming."

Jacob nods. Moves toward the far end of the hall where shadows still cling to the corners.

He moves the mop the floorboards. Back and forth. Push and pull. His mind wanders as his body works. Thinking of all the kicks and jabs and chops the kids who train here use.

He glances at his mother. She's on her hands and knees, scrubbing the area beneath the weapons rack where sweat and dirt accumulate most. Her hair is pulled back in a tight ponytail. No makeup. She should get one of those nanites that smooths her skin out. But they can't afford even the lowest of levels. Not even an EverFresh.

The skin around her knuckles is cracked from chemical cleaners and constant immersion in water. Two jobs—dojo in the morning, diner in the afternoon—and still they live in a shelter.

"You have school today?" she asks without looking up.

"It's summer, Mom."

"Right." She nods, moving to the next section of floor. "You should get a summer job then. The convenience store on Pike has a sign up."

Jacob tightens his grip on the mop handle. "Master Han said he might let me help with the kids' class."

His mom pauses scrubbing for a fraction of a second. "We'll see."

We'll see. The answer that isn't an answer. Jacob returns to his mopping, gripping the handle so tight he almost snaps it in half.

Morning light soars through the windows, punching holes in the shadows. The rows of practice dummies stand at attention along one wall, their fabric bodies bearing the scars of countless strikes. Punching bags' hang from reinforced ceiling mounts. The wall-mounted weapons—staffs, practice swords, nunchaku—cast thin shadows like prison bars across the gleaming floor.

Jacob has memorized every centimeter of this space without ever formally training in it. Two years of watching from the sidelines, observing through the crack in the door while completing his chores. Learning from the whispers.

His mother thinks he doesn't see how Master Han looks at him sometimes. The calculating gaze, measuring his height, his reach, the way he moves even when just carrying cleaning supplies. Jacob pretends not to notice, but he is secretly pleased. Secretly waiting for the invitation to join the other kids on the mats.

A muscle in Jacob's arm twitches, wanting to move through the forms he's secretly memorized. *Not now.* His mother would see.

How many students take this place for granted? How many complain about the training, never realizing what a privilege it is to be here as something other than the help?

His mom rises from her knees with a barely audible groan. Jacob pretends not to hear it. Her pride is a fragile thing, and he's learned when to look away.

"The bathrooms next," she says, gathering her supplies. "Then we dust the trophy case."

The trophy case. Glass-fronted, spotlit, dominated by Master Han's achievements. Tournament cups, medals, certificates—all bearing his name in gleaming gold letters. Pride of place goes to the World Championship trophy from fifteen years ago. Master Han making history as the first Korean American to take the title.

"I'm almost done here," Jacob says, pushing the mop into the final corner.

His mom nods, disappearing into the changing rooms with her bucket and scrub brush. The door swings shut behind her.

Alone, Jacob allows himself a single glance at his reflection in the mirrored wall. Thirteen, tall for his age, with his father's build and his mother's dark eyes. The man who left before Jacob could remember him still exists in the angles of Jacob's jaw, the set of his shoulders.

He looks away. Reflection is a luxury he can't afford, not when there's so much work to be done.

By the time they finish, every surface gleams. Every weapon sits perfectly aligned. The air smells of pine cleaner and furniture polish. His eyes linger on the center of the room—the heart of the dojo where Master Han demonstrates forms to his advanced students. The space where champions are made.

His mother's voice echoes from the women's changing room as she hums a half-remembered Korean lullaby while scrubbing sinks. He has maybe fifteen minutes before she returns. Fifteen minutes when the floor belongs to no one but him.

He takes three cautious steps backward. One more glance at the changing room door. Still closed. One more check of the entrance. Still empty.

His heart kicks against his ribs. This is stupid. Dangerous. If Master Han caught him—

But Master Han won't be here for another hour. And Jacob's body hums with a familiar restlessness.

He peels off his socks, tucks them into his pocket. Bare

feet against the floor. He moves to the center of the training space, standing where Master Han always begins demonstrations. The mirrors reflect his lanky frame from three angles.

Jacob steadies his breathing. In through the nose, out through the mouth. Just like he's observed the senior students do. He brings his hands together, centers himself, then slides his right foot back into the first stance.

Basic form first. Nothing flashy. He sinks into a horse stance, thighs parallel to the ground, back straight. His arms extend in a double block. He holds it, feeling the burn start in his quadriceps, the strain across his shoulders.

Ten seconds. Twenty. Thirty. The stance settles into his muscles, becoming easier with each breath.

He transitions to the next position, a front stance with a middle punch. He snaps his fist forward. The air parts around his knuckles with a soft whisper.

It's not his first time practicing. It's just his first time here, in the sacred center of the dojo, rather than in the cramped confines of the shelter bathroom, the only place with a mirror and enough privacy.

Jacob moves through the beginner's Kata. Each movement flows into the next, a river finding its course. He's watched the white belts perform this routine hundreds of times while dusting or carrying supplies. Has mentally mapped every step, every turn, every strike.

His reflection catches his eye. Not perfect. His elbow drifts too high on the knife-hand strike. His weight shifts too far forward in the back stance. But not bad. Not bad at all for someone who's never had a single lesson.

Sweat beads at his temples as he completes the sequence. The Kata ends with a formal bow, hands at his sides, eyes lowered. When he straightens, he knows he's not finished. He wants more.

Jacob shifts into the intermediate form he's memorized from watching the green belts. This one has faster transitions, higher kicks, sharper turns. His body responds with surprising willingness, as though it's been waiting for this moment.

The rhythm of the movements carries him forward. Block, strike, turn, kick. For these precious minutes, he isn't the cleaner's son. He isn't the kid who sleeps on a cot in the middle of a shelter. He's finding his purpose.

Three minutes pass. Five. He loses track of time as he progresses to elements of the advanced forms. This is where his memorization gets spotty. He's only glimpsed these sequences through doorways or while pretending to sweep nearby.

Jacob experiments with a spinning kick, turning his body and extending his leg in a sweeping arc. Not quite right. He tries again, adjusting the angle of his hips, the position of his supporting foot.

Better.

On the third attempt, he slices his leg through the air with enough force to create a soft whoosh. The kick would have connected perfectly with the shadow on the far wall if he'd been aiming for it.

He grins. This is what it's all about.

Jacob lands and immediately springs into the next movement—a high crescent kick that transitions into a low sweep.

It's from the black belt form, the most advanced sequence performed in the dojo. He's never seen it performed in its entirety, only in fragments during Master Han's private sessions with his top students.

He's mid-extension, his leg at its highest point, when a shadow shifts at the entrance.

Jacob freezes. Muscle memory screams to complete the motion, but shock holds him in place like a statue.

Master Han Seo stands in the doorway. He doesn't speak. Doesn't move. Just watches with eyes that miss nothing.

The silence stretches between them, tight as a bowstring.

Then, footsteps. His Mom's quick stride approaches from the changing rooms. Jacob finally breaks from his suspended kick, lowering his leg with an ungraceful thump as his mother returns to the main hall.

She catches him in motion—not cleaning, not working, but standing in the center of the training area. Her eyes narrow immediately, darting between her son and the master of the dojo.

"Back to work," she whispers, her voice carrying an urgency that makes Jacob wince. She crosses to him in four quick steps and puts a gentle hand on his arm, pushing downward as though physically returning him to his place.

The heat of embarrassment crawls up Jacob's neck.

Master Han steps fully into the dojo, his posture rigid and commanding. Light catches on the silver threads in his black hair, on the embroidered dragon on his traditional jacket. His face remains impassive, but his eyes—his eyes are glued to Jacob.

His mom bows her head. Jacob follows her lead with a quick, reluctant dip of his own.

"Mrs. Shea," Master Han says, his voice carrying the faint accent that twenty years in America hasn't erased. "The changing rooms are clean?"

"Yes, Master Han," she answers, eyes still lowered. "Just finished."

"Good." His gaze shifts to Jacob, lingers. Something flickers in the older man's expression—interest, perhaps. Or opportunity. "And your son helps you today."

It isn't a question, but she answers anyway. "Yes. School break."

Master Han nods once, sharply, then moves toward his office. Before entering, he pauses, looking back at Jacob over his shoulder.

"Your form," he says, "needs work."

The door closes behind him with a definitive click.

His Mom digs her fingers into Jacob's forearm. "What were you thinking?" she hisses, keeping her voice low. "You want us to lose this job? Do you want us to get out of the shelter?"

"He didn't seem angry," Jacob replies, his eyes still on Master Han's closed door.

"That's worse." She releases his arm and bends to retrieve her cleaning bucket. "He doesn't get angry. He calculates."

Jacob's pulse thrums at his throat. Not from fear or exertion now, but from a dangerous kind of hope. Master Han saw him. *Really* saw him.

Something has shifted. The air feels different against his skin. The space feels different around his body.

For those few minutes, he belonged here. And Master Han saw it too.

To carry on reading, click here:
https://geni.us/JacobShea